THE ALIEN FIRE FILE

The Alien Fire File
A Hunter and Moon Mystery

Allan Frewin Jones

Hodder
Children's
Books

a division of Hodder Headline plc

A Catalogue record for this book is available from
the British Library

ISBN 0 340 67819 4

Typeset by Palimpsest Book Production Limited,
Polmont, Stirlingshire
Printed and bound in Great Britain by
Cox & Wyman Ltd, Reading, Berks.

Hodder Children's Books
a division of Hodder Headline plc
338 Euston Road
London NW1 3BH

1

Beth Hunter woke up with a start.

She had been dreaming about huge octopus-type things that glowed with a horrible green light. They were surging through the night on massive slithery tentacles in search of human prey.

They had risen from the sea and now they were everywhere. They throbbed with radioactivity and made a constant maddening high-pitched screeching noise.

One of the octopus-things coiled a tentacle around Beth's physical fitness teacher and bit him in half with one *snick* of its deadly, snapping beak-like mouth-parts.

Yessss! Beth thought, even in her dream, *Way to go, octopus!* She had never liked that guy.

Then Hal's heroic older brother, Joe, had come roaring up on his motorbike to save them all. But one of the octopus-things had spotted him and had stretched out a slithery tentacle toward him.

'Joe!' Beth had screamed. 'Watch out!'

And then she woke up.

Her window blind was glowing with a creepy green light and she could hear a weird clicking, buzzing, wailing noise coming from outside her window.

No, no, no, she said to herself, *this isn't happening!* She scrunched her eyes tight shut and slammed her hands over her ears. *This is one of those wierdo dreams where you THINK you've woken up, but you haven't really. THAT's what's going on here. I'm still asleep.*

She took a few deep, calming breaths then opened her eyes again.

Oh, heck!

It was all still there. The green light and the freaky noise. And the green light was sliding around on her blind, rippling and getting brighter and dimmer through the thin material.

What should she do? Mom's bedroom was at the front of the house, and so was Gran's. Beth had insisted on a bedroom in back so that she could wake up every morning and see the ocean.

She hadn't planned on being sucked out of her bed in the middle of the night by some octopus-monster-thing. That wasn't part of the deal *at all*!

She had to prove to herself that she was

2

still asleep. What did people do? They pinched themselves.

Why?

Because if it hurts, that proves you're awake, dumbo.

Oh, right. Here goes, then.

Beth pinched her arm really hard.

'Ow!' She rubbed her arm. 'OK, so this isn't a dream.' She tried to keep calm while her brain raced through the possibilities.

Go fetch Mom.

Hide under the bed until morning.

Scream your head off!

She nearly jumped clean out of her pyjamas as her window rattled with some kind of impact from outside. But it wasn't the disgusting, squooshy, squodgy kind of noise you'd expect from a radioactive mutant tentacle. It was a hard, sharp sound. Like pebbles thrown up at the glass.

In the immediate aftermath of the noise, the green light faded and the hissing, wailing quietened down, as if whatever was out there was moving away from the house.

Beth bounded out of bed and ran to the window. She yanked on the cord and the blind snaked up with a dry rustle.

'Oh, my gosh!' Beth could only stare in disbelief

at the sight that met her eyes down in the long back yard. Way down at the end, about twenty yards away where the bushes bordered the beach road, a thick smear of green smoke crept across the grass like some kind of supernatural fog.

But what on earth *was* it?

Beth was no coward. If there was something bizarre going on, then she wanted to know what it was. Green lights, green smoke, uncanny noises. What did it all add up to?

She threw her robe on and ran for the door.

She raced along the hall to her mother's room.

'Mom! Mom!' Beth shook her. The way her mom slept made the average log seem like an insomniac. 'Mom! Wake up!'

'What?' At last! Her mom rolled over in bed. She blinked in the glare of the bedside light that Beth had switched on. 'Beth? What's the matter?'

'There's stuff out back,' Beth panted. 'Green stuff. Giant octopuses.' Still woozy from sleep, Beth was getting confused. 'No, I don't mean giant octopuses. Green smoke and stuff. And a weird noise.' She yanked at her mother's arm. 'Mom, you gotta come see! Please!'

Mrs Hunter could tell that Beth was serious. Whatever she *thought* she'd seen out there, it had certainly scared her.

'OK, OK, I'm coming, honey. No need to pull my arm off.'

Beth was dragging her mother across the floor almost before she had time to wrap her robe around herself.

'What was that about octopuses?'

'Huh?'

'You mentioned giant octopuses.'

'No, I didn't.'

'Beth! If this is just another of your screwy dreams!'

'It isn't. Cross my heart, I *saw* it!'

Mrs Hunter switched on the hall light and Beth ran down the stairs, hauling her mother along in her wake.

'Don't turn the light on!' Beth said as they went into the kitchen. 'It'll *see*!'

'*What* will see?'

'I don't know. *It*!' Beth leaped to the window and lifted the blind an inch or two. She peered out into the dark of the night.

'Well?' Mrs Hunter asked.

'Uh . . .'

Mrs Hunter unlocked the back door and swung it open. The cool night air of the New England fall came breathing into the kitchen, heavy with the smell of the Atlantic Ocean.

Mrs Hunter stepped out on to the wooden deck.

Beth followed her, the breeze ruffling the long tangled red curls that hung loose over her shoulders.

Mrs Hunter looked into Beth's pale, freckly face.

'Well?' she said again, sounding a little annoyed this time.

Beth walked to the edge of the deck. Her green eyes stared into the darkness of the cloudy night.

There were no green lights. There was no creeping green smoke. And there were no spooky noises. The night was as quiet and as still as only a small town in the middle of the countryside can ever be. The only sound to disturb the stillness was the sibilant hiss of waves on the nearby beach.

Beth looked around at her mom.

'I saw something,' she said. 'Definitely.'

Her mom gave her a withering look then turned and disappeared back into the house. Mrs Hunter didn't say a *word*. She didn't need to. Beth knew exactly what was going through her mom's mind.

Why was I cursed with a daughter with the most

over-active imagination in the whole of the United States of America? Why ME?

Beth sighed. *This is the story of my life*, she thought to herself as she wandered miserably back into the kitchen. *I see stuff and I hear stuff that no one else ever hears or sees, and then they wind up thinking I'm some kind of nut. I wish, I really do wish, just for once that this kind of thing would happen to someone else!*

But it was no good wishing that. Beth Hunter attracted weirdness like honey attracts wasps, and that was just the plain, honest truth of the matter!

First thing next morning, Beth hauled on a pair of jeans and a sweater and set off through the dew-drenched grass to go visit Hal. At least *he* would take her seriously.

As Beth made her way down the front lawn to the road, she heard a tapping sound from behind her. She looked around. Gran was waving from her bedroom window. Beth waved back. Her gran started performing some weird kind of mime with her arms.

Beth stopped to watch, grinning as her gran's arms waved around behind the glass.

Finally Beth figured out what her gran was

trying to tell her. It was going to *rain*. The old lady's frantic mime had been of someone getting wet and wishing they'd remembered an umbrella. Only gran would try miming someone *forgetting* an umbrella! Beth was totally convinced that her gran was the loopiest, most amazing gran a person ever had. She had been born in Romania, in Eastern Europe, and had arrived at Ellis Island, New York, when she was only ten years old. But somehow the strange culture of her homeland had never really left her, and there were times when Beth couldn't make head nor tail of what her gran was talking about, even though the old lady spoke perfect English.

Sharing a house with her gran was one of the things that made life so perfect for Beth. That, and the fact that the little fishing port of New Greenwich was the most wonderful place on earth. Bar none!

Beth and her mom had been living there for some months now. The two of them had moved from their apartment in the suburbs of New York City when Beth's mom had been promoted from Police Sergeant to Lieutenant and taken a transfer to a post in Boston.

Beth's father had died when she was only two years old. Gran was the only other family Beth and her mom had. Not that self-sufficient, inquisitive Beth felt the need for a whole bunch of aunts and uncles and cousins and stuff. Her down-to-earth, practical mom and her off-beat gran were all the people Beth needed.

Apart from her new friend, Hal Moon. Hal was twelve, the same age as Beth, except that his birthday was September 13th – which made him exactly three days younger than Beth. And that was a fact she didn't let him ever forget.

The Moon family lived next door to the Hunters. But where Beth's house was old and built of whitewashed stone, the Moons' home was a modern, clapboard house. Both houses backed on to the beach road, and beyond the road, across a narrow strip of scrubland, lay the long, golden beaches of Monasaukee Bay and the dark, rolling waters of the Atlantic Ocean.

If a person wanted to find New Greenwich, they'd have to take the road north from Boston. They'd need to drive along the Massachusetts coast until they came to that place where New Hampshire edges its way out under the long, jagged coastline of Maine. Then they should follow the quietest, most deserted roads through the lush, green New England farmlands for forty miles, and take the fork to the right. Pretty soon they'd see the peaceful, quaint old town nestling up against the sweeping curve of Monasaukee Bay, and – if they had Beth's heart – they would fall in love with the town at first sight.

Just the way Beth had fallen in love with the two hundred year-old house with its tall white walls and its unkempt yard and its long, sunbleached deck where a person could sit in a lawn-chair and gaze out over the ocean to Cranberry Island and beyond.

Beth looked up. Heavy white clouds towered up into the sky like molten mountains, moving slowly eastwards. But to the west the clouds were getting darker.

She waved Gran goodbye and trotted down to the road and off to Hal's place.

She stepped carefully over the scattered pieces of Joe Moon's motorbike. She avoided treading on little Ben's toys as she mounted the steps to the front door.

Before she had time to ring the bell, the front door opened like a jack-in-the-box and Hal stood there grinning at her.

'Listen,' Beth said without even pausing to say *hi*. 'I saw the most amazing stuff last night. You're just not going to believe me.'

Hal brushed his limp, pale brown hair off his

face and gazed at her with his big puppy-dog brown eyes.

'I always make it a point to believe something amazing before breakfast,' he said. 'Especially if you're going to tell me that you saw weird green lights last night and heard strange noises.'

Beth stared at him. 'How do you know that?'

Hal gave her a strange, knowing look. 'Because you're not the only person who saw them,' he intoned solemnly.

'Huh?'

Hal leaned toward her and whispered in her ear. 'UFOs.'

'*What*?'

'Unidentified flying objects,' Hal said. 'Come on in and I'll tell you what *I* saw.'

Beth followed him breathlessly into the house, her mystery antennae all atwitch in anticipation of the revelations Hal was about to make.

2

Usually when Beth visited Hal's house, their first stop-off was in the kitchen to raid the refrigerator, but this time he led her straight up to his room. Once inside he carefully closed the door. He listened for a moment or two at the wooden panels.

'What're you doing?' Beth asked.

'Checking that no one's listening,' Hal hissed.

Beth sat down on his bed. 'Like *who*?'

'Like *the unknown*,' Hal said in a strange voice. Beth felt a shiver run down her spine.

'Cut that out!' she said. 'I wanna know how you know I saw all that strange stuff last night. And I wanna know what you mean by *UFOs*.'

'I told you,' Hal said. 'Unidentified flying objects.'

'I know what it *means*,' Beth said impatiently. 'I want to know what *you* mean. Will you get away from that door? Who's going to listen in on us: Ben?' Ben was Hal's toddler brother. Beth's opinion of little kids was that they should all be put on an island somewhere away from normal folk until they started acting *human*.

'You can't be too careful,' Hal said as he came across the room and threw himself on to the bed. 'Aliens can do all kinds of seriously freaky stuff, Beth.'

'Quit it with the aliens,' Beth said uneasily. 'Tell me: who else saw the green lights last night?'

'*I* did,' Hal said. '*And* I saw where the lights were coming from.' Hal pointed toward the long picture-window of his room. Like Beth's, Hal's bedroom overlooked the ocean. 'I woke up when I heard this strange, buzzing, whining noise.'

'I heard that, too.'

'Uh-huh?'

'Yeah. And a green light shone right on my window.'

'Yup.' Hal nodded. 'Mine, too. But I bet you didn't jump out of bed like I did. I bet you didn't check it out. I bet you didn't see what I saw.'

'I did check it out,' Beth said. 'But all I saw was some weird green smoke. Except that it didn't act like smoke. It was kind of creeping along the grass at the bottom of the back yard.' She gave Hal a sharp look. 'What did you see?'

'It was hovering out there,' Hal said, lifting his arm toward the window and making his hand tremble flat in the air. 'Hovering just above the water.'

Beth put her hands to her mouth. 'Not giant octopuses,' she said. 'Tell me you didn't see giant octopuses.'

Hal stared at her. 'Giant octopuses? Where did you get giant octopuses from?'

'I was dreaming about giant octopuses,' Beth explained. 'Giant green octopuses. One of them ate Mr Wisdon. It cut him in two with one bite. It was great! And then your brother came along the road on his motorbike, and—'

'Beth!' Hal interrupted. 'Can you shut up about giant octopuses for a second? I saw a spaceship!'

'*No!*' Beth's eyes were as round as saucers. If she'd opened them one squidgeon wider, they'd probably have popped clean out of their sockets and bounced down into her lap.

'Yes.'

'You didn't!' Beth gasped in awe.

'I did, I did!'

'Hal, Moon, you total, utter and complete *rat!*' Beth yelled. For a moment, Hal thought Beth was going to fly at him with fists flailing like helicopter blades. Red-haired Beth was quite capable of bursts of fiery temper, as Hal had discovered to his cost in the past.

14

'What did I do?' Hal yelped as he ducked out of reach of Beth's long, skinny arms.

'All my life, *all my entire life*, I've been dying to see a spaceship,' Beth hollered. 'And I've never seen one. Never! Not even an itsy-bitsy little glimpse of one! How *dare* you go around seeing spaceships without me, Hal Moon! What do you think you're playing at?'

Hal had wondered how Beth might react to his story. As usual, Beth came up with a reaction he hadn't figured on.

'Calm down,' Hal said. 'I mean, it wasn't like they dropped by for cookies and a coke. I only saw the ship for a split second.' Hal drew a swift arc through the air with an outstretched finger that almost hit Beth on the nose. 'It went, like: schwooooom-kerzzzzip, really, really fast. And then it was gone.'

'You said it was hovering.'

'No, I didn't.'

'You did, too,' Beth said. 'You said it was hovering over the water.'

'Oh, yeah. Right.'

'So? Was it hovering or was it schwoooom-kerzzzziping?'

'Both,' Hal said quickly. 'It *schwoomed* first, then it hovered for a second or two, then it *kerzippped*

15

right up into the sky until it looked no bigger than a lightning bug, and then it vanished completely.'

'Oh, wow,' Beth breathed. 'That is just so *phenomenally* brilliant. And I guess the lights were kind of . . . searchlights. I guess they were taking a real good look at us.' She frowned. 'Hey, do you think those guys would have the kind of technology that would allow them to see clean through walls and stuff?'

'Beth, they came here from another planet,' Hal said. 'Sure they can see through walls. Those guys can probably read a person's mind.' Hal warmed to the subject. 'Heck, they've probably got a special ray-gun type machine that homes in on your brain.' He waggled a stretched-out finger an inch from Beth's wrinkled forehead. 'And then sucks your thoughts clean out of your skull. Schloop! And then they keep your thoughts and your memories and everything in a special computer on board the ship.' Hal's voice lowered to a hoarse whisper. 'And back here on earth you'd be acting like a total *zombie*, because your brain is in outer space.' He grinned suddenly. 'Not that people would notice much difference in your case.'

'Oh, ha, ha,' Beth said. 'You're about as funny as food poisoning at Thanksgiving.'

'Why did you want to know if they could see through walls?' Hal asked.

'I was in my *pyjamas*!' Beth said indignantly. 'I don't want some nosey jerk from outer space seeing me in my pyjamas.'

'They're just collecting *data*,' Hal said. 'Listen, as far as they're concerned we're just like *bugs*. Them watching us is just like us watching the ants in the ant-colony at school. They shine their green light, and suck up all the information they need. Then they go off somewhere quiet and figure it all out.'

'Do you think they're gonna *invade* us once they've gotten all the information they need?' Beth said.

'I don't think so,' Hal said. 'But I think they might *abduct* some people. If you ask me, they shine their green light to check things out, and then the next thing they do is to suck someone up into their spaceship to experiment on them. I've read all about that kind of thing in books, Beth. People see a bright light in the sky and then they go unconscious, and when they wake up again it's *hours* or even *days* later. I read about one girl who lived right near here, in a little town called Darkwood. She went missing for ten years. She was abducted when she was twelve years old and she didn't turn up again until she was twenty-two.'

'I'm twelve,' Beth said.

Hal nodded. 'Exactly!'

'Oh, heck, we've got to *tell* someone about this.'

'Huh!' Hal snorted. 'Who's gonna believe us? They don't even believe it when grown ups say they've seen UFOs, never mind people our age.'

'I don't care,' Beth said. 'I'm gonna tell everyone! Look, here's the thing: we can't have been the only people to have seen those lights. And maybe someone else saw the spaceship out there. I'm going to tell my mom. I'm going to call the newspapers. I'm going to call the police. The mayor. The state governor. And I'm gonna keep right on calling people until someone believes me.'

'Now hold on, Beth . . .'

'And you're going to help me, Hal. You're going to tell them exactly what you saw.'

'Wait up!' Hal almost yelled. 'I really don't think that's a very good idea, Beth. Seriously!'

But Beth wasn't listening. 'I'm gonna see if I can find the phone number of one of those groups of people who investigate this kind of thing. You know, those guys who check up on paranormal outer-space type stuff. We can tell them all about the green lights and the smoke and they can come and check the place out for . . . uh, traces of outer-space-type radiation-stuff. *They'll* know we're not just making it up!'

Beth jumped up off the bed. 'Where do you keep your telephone directories?'

'Beth, let's think about this before we do anything crazy.'

'What's to think about?' Beth said. 'I saw the lights. You saw the spaceship. Let's go tell people. Even if they don't believe us *now*, at least they'll know we were telling the truth if we get abducted.'

Beth didn't wait for any more arguments from Hal. She ran to the door and grabbed the handle. But the handle wouldn't turn.

'Hal? Did you lock this door?' she asked as she struggled to twist the reluctant handle.

'Nope. Why?'

'I can't get it to . . . oh! Oh! Ohhhh!' The handle seemed suddenly to have taken on a life of its own. It began to turn in Beth's fingers.

'Beth! Let go the handle, can't you!' It was Mr Moon's voice from the other side of the door. Beth released the handle as if it had become red hot. The door opened and Mr Moon stood staring down at her.

Beth grinned up at him. 'We must've both taken hold at the same time,' she said. Don Moon was a very tall, very thin, very gaunt man with long, swept back black hair and deep, dark eyes. He always made Beth think of a mad scientist in a monster movie. And Don Moon actually *did* work for the movies. He was a special effects wizard.

'Hiya, Beth,' Mr Moon said with the particular smile he always used on her. A smile that said: she's as crazy as a coyote, but I kind of like her.

'Hi, Mr Moon,' Beth said.

'Hal? I need those things back you borrowed, son.'

'Oh, right. I'll let you have them in a little while, Dad,' Hal said.

'I need them now,' Mr Moon said. 'I have to be at the shoot tonight and I need to take my gear with me. It's going to take all day to get there.'

'Are you starting a new movie?' Beth asked.

'I sure am, Beth,' Mr Moon said. 'They're shooting it over in Vermont. Hasn't Hal told you about it? It's a sci-fi movie. It's called *The Abduction*. It's all about aliens abducting people and kookie stuff like that.'

'It's all about *what*?' Beth growled, glaring

at Hal with a sudden suspicion dawning in her mind.

'I guess you're in a hurry, Dad,' Hal gabbled as he leaped off the bed. 'You go finish packing the car and I'll bring the stuff down to you.'

'OK, son,' Mr Moon said. He turned to go but then paused. 'Oh, by the way, have you been messing with my smoke pots? There's a green one missing from the workshop.'

'Hold everything!' Beth yelled, now *very* suspicious indeed. 'What exactly is a green smoke pot?'

'It's one of my special effects doo-das,' Mr Moon said. 'You light the fuse and a whole load of dense green smoke comes creeping out like a thick fog. They'll want plenty of that kind of thing in *The Abduction*.' Mr Moon didn't notice the ferocious expression on Beth's face. Hal did.

'I can explain,' Hal said.

'Explain what?' Mr Moon asked.

'I'm gonna *kill* you!' Beth screamed at Hal as he ducked behind the bed. 'UFOs! It was *you*! There was never any spaceship! You set the whole thing up to make a monkey out of me! I'm gonna kill you stone dead, Hal Moon!'

3

For five whole days Beth totally ignored Hal. In homeroom at school she even moved to a desk on the other side of the class from him so she could ignore him from as far away as possible. In the school cafeteria she sat at full tables so there was no room for him to come creeping up alongside her.

Hal tried really hard to make up to her. But when Beth Hunter was mad at a person, she *stayed* mad. And Beth was *mad*.

Hal couldn't figure out why she'd reacted so badly. After all, it wasn't like this was the first time he'd played a practical joke on her. Hal was famous for his practical jokes. Sure, Beth would sometimes get mad when she realised what was going on, but then she'd cool off and they'd be friends again. But *this* time it looked to Hal like she was never going to speak to him again.

And like people say: if looks could kill, Hal Moon would have been history!

It turned out that the green light had been a

powerful flashlight with a green filter over it. The weird noises were from a sci-fi special effects tape played through a portable cassette machine. Hal had shone the light up on her bedroom window from down on the deck. Then he'd thrown a handful of pebbles up at the window to make sure she woke up. The creepy smoke had been one of Mr Moon's special effects smoke pots hidden in the bushes at the bottom of Beth's garden. The whole thing had been set up by Hal as a joke.

Except that Beth hadn't seen the funny side of it.

Not at all, she hadn't!

On the way home from school on Friday afternoon, Hal tried to make up with Beth one more time.

'Hiya!' he said, running to catch up with her as she stalked along the road that led to their houses. 'How's it going?'

'Drop dead.'

Hal gave her a cheerful grin. 'You don't mean that.'

'Wanna bet?' She speeded up so that he had to walk really fast to keep up with her.

'How long are you going to keep this up, Beth?' he asked. 'I said I was sorry.'

'I'm not talking to you.'

'Yes, you are. You just did!'

'I am not!' Beth snapped. 'And I'm never going to speak to you again. And that's a promise.'

Hal stopped in his tracks. He gazed at Beth as she marched away from him on her long, skinny legs. Her great unruly mass of flame-red hair was tied in its usual thick bunch at her neck, the curls reaching half way down her back.

'Help,' Hal called out, clutching his chest. 'I'm having a coronary! Arrgh! Beth! Help!' He crumpled to his knees and slumped sideways to fall in a heap in the road.

'Good!' she yelled back without looking around.

Hal sat up. 'Think how you'd feel if something bad really did happen to me,' he shouted at her receding back. 'I bet you'd feel just awful!'

It didn't work. Beth just carried right on walking. If Hal was going to make friends with her, he was going to have to try a whole lot harder than that.

'Hiya, Gran,' Beth called as she closed the front door behind her and slung her school bag into a dark corner of the hallway. 'What's cooking?'

The hall was thick with the mouthwatering smell of baking.

'Hello, Beth,' Gran called from the kitchen. 'How was your day?'

Beth walked into the kitchen. 'So-so,' she said. 'I had . . . to . . .' Her voice faded as she stared at the uproar all around her. It was as if every knife, plate, bowl, spoon, whisk, cup, saucer and cook-pot had been used and then just left where it had fallen. And the table was awash with spills of flour and cocoa-powder and blobs of butter and coagulated pools of egg white.

And in the midst of all this utter chaos, Beth's gran was sitting in her wooden armchair with her feet up on the table, an open book in one hand and a thick slice of some gooey brown cake in the other.

'Gran, what have you been *doing*?' Beth gasped.

'I needed to bake Ugly Cake,' Gran said with a chocolatey grin. 'Sometimes I just need to bake Ugly Cake. Try some. It's the cat's pyjamas, I'm telling you!'

Beth looked at the cake. It was kind of flat and square and lumpy and totally smothered in a chocolate sauce as thick and knobbly as tarmac. One big slice was missing. The rest of it had oozed into the gap like a mudslide.

'Ugly Cake?' Beth said. 'Gran, why is it called Ugly Cake?'

Her gran laughed. 'Take a look. Tell me if that isn't the ugliest cake you've ever seen. Try some, Beth. Anyone would think I'd baked a snake from the look on your face.'

Beth cut herself a slice of cake and tried it out with a spoon. Surprisingly, it tasted delicious. Sweet and creamy and nutty and chocolatey. Beth cleared a few things off a chair and sat down.

'What's in it?'

'It's an old recipe,' Gran said. 'Very secret. I'll tell you when you come of age.'

'When will that be?'

'One day soon, I guess,' Gran said.

Out in the hall, the telephone rang.

Gran brought her feet down off the table with a bang and stood up. 'I'll get it,' she said. 'You enjoy your cake.'

A moment or two later her head appeared around the door. 'It's Hal.'

'Tell him to go boil his head.'

Beth listened to her gran's voice. 'Beth says you should go boil your head, Hal. Oh. Right. Just a second.' Gran called to Beth. 'Hal says how long should he boil it for?'

Beth couldn't help a splutter of laughter. 'Tell him ten years!'

Gran spoke into the phone again. 'Yeah, sure. OK. I'll tell her. Goodbye.'

She came back into the kitchen. 'Look at all this mess,' she said, as if she'd only just seen it. 'It's like under the sofa at Rudi's in here! Your mother will have kittens.'

'This cake is amazing,' Beth mumbled through a sticky, gooey mouthful. 'Don't worry about the mess, I'll help you clear up. It's hours before Mom gets home. What did Hal say?'

'He said to tell you he's really sorry he upset you.'

'Yeah, *well*!' Beth grumbled.

Gran sat down and put an arm around Beth's shoulders.

'So, why are you so mad at him, Beth? He's always making jokes, but you've never been mad at him for this long before.'

'This is different,' Beth said. She looked into her gran's kind, wrinkled old face. 'I know it sounds totally dumb, but I really wanted it to be something from another planet out there that night.' Beth's gran knew all about the elaborate trick Hal had played. 'I really wanted it to have been aliens. I've always wanted to meet up with an alien. Well, maybe not *meet* one, but *see* one. Loads of people see UFOs, and I never do. And

27

I really thought maybe at last I'd really, truly seen something from outer space.' Beth growled angrily. 'And it was that stupid, idiotic, dumb, *infant* Hal all along!'

Gran gave her a curious look.

'I think you're better off not seeing aliens,' she said.

'What makes you say that?' Beth asked.

'Who'd believe you?' Gran said with a shrug. 'People would just say it was make-believe. Trust me.'

There was something in her gran's voice that made Beth look closely at her.

'Gran?' she said cautiously. 'Have you ever—'

'Now then,' Gran interrupted. 'When are you going to forgive Hal, hmm?'

'Not just yet,' Beth said.

Gran smiled. 'You're going to make him suffer a little first?'

'Darned right. But—'

Gran looked around the kitchen. 'I guess we'd better start clearing up in here.'

They cleaned up the whole of the kitchen before Beth's mom got home from Boston. And Mrs Hunter wouldn't have known anything about the mess if she hadn't sat in a blob of cocoa-butter at dinner time that Beth and her gran had missed.

Beth's mom stood up and twisted around to look at the gooey brown squelch on the back of her skirt. She glared at Gran.

'Mom! You've been making Ugly Cake again!'

'You always liked my Ugly Cake,' Gran said with a smile.

'Not to sit in, I didn't!'

Beth was nearly killing herself trying not to laugh. Then her mom started laughing, too.

'You'd better have left me some, that's all!' she said as she headed out of the kitchen to change her skirt.

Early on Saturday morning the telephone rang. Beth had just come in from a walk on the beach, her trainers gritty with damp sand and saturated with dew from the long grass. She was making the most of these long, golden fall days. Gran had told her that when winter hit New Greenwich, it hit hard.

But there were still a couple of months to go before the trees lost their brown and red and deep yellow mantle of leaves. And Beth loved her solitary walks through the foaming surf in the early morning when the sky was streaked with such amazing colours that you'd think someone had gone crazy with a whole pallet of paints.

She scooped up the phone. 'Hello?'

'Beth, it's Hal. Don't hang up on me.'

Beth felt really peaceful after her walk on the beach. Maybe it was something to do with the calming effects of the tangy air that came fresh off the ocean. She thought maybe she was about ready to forgive Hal. He'd learned his lesson.

'What do you want?' she asked.

'Can you come over? Something's happened and I really need to talk to you about it.'

'So, talk,' Beth said, sitting on the stairs. 'I'm listening.' There was a long pause from the other end. 'Hal? You there?'

'Yes, I'm here. I don't want to talk about it on the phone.' Hal's voice certainly sounded odd.

'Is something wrong?' Beth asked, suddenly anxious. 'What's happened?'

'Promise you won't hang up?'

'For heaven's sake, Hal!'

'Promise!'

'OK. I promise.'

There was another pause. Then Hal's voice came over the phone, sounding totally spooked.

'I was thirsty last night,' he said. 'I got up for a drink of water. And I looked out of my bedroom window. Beth, you've gotta believe me. I saw the *freakiest* thing. Way out in the bay, over near Cranberry Island. I saw a really, really weird green light out there. I—'

Beth slammed the phone down so hard she nearly broke it in two.

The nerve of that guy, trying the same stupid stunt *twice*! Did he think she was a total moron, or what?

Beth stamped upstairs to her room.

'Who was that on the phone, honey?' her mom called from the bathroom.

'No one!' Beth snapped. 'No one *at all*!'

4

If Hal so much as showed his *nose* anywhere near her, Beth was totally prepared to bite it clean off! The fact that he was always playing stupid jokes was something she could forgive: the guy couldn't help it. And the fact that he'd tricked her over something that had really gotten to her was *almost* forgiveable. But that he should think she was so dumb as to fall for the same brainless scam *twice in a row*! Now, *that* was really annoying.

She was still fuming when she sat down to breakfast with her mom and her gran.

'It looks like we might be having a little trouble around here,' Mrs Hunter said from behind *The Clarion*, the local newspaper. 'Seventh Wave are picketing Webcore again.'

Webcore was a large chemicals factory some miles up-state. Beth had heard about them before, usually when the environmental group, Seventh Wave appeared on TV with an expose about how Webcore and other local firms were polluting the environment.

'Huh! They should go picket Hal Moon,' Beth muttered. 'He's more trouble around here than any factory!'

Her mom peered at her over the newspaper.

'Still mad at him, huh?'

'You *bet* I am!'

Beth didn't see Hal all the rest of that day. But he left her a trail of messages.

The first one was taped to the mailbox out front. It just said: *Beth! It's true! Honest!* Beth scrunched it up and threw it in the trash can.

Later that morning she took a walk down to The Front. The Front was the most touristy part of New Greenwich. It was old-fashioned and just a little shabby here and there where the old fishing huts had fallen into disrepair; but it had modern restaurants and a whole bunch of antique shops and craft-stores and galleries where local artists and craftspeople displayed and sold their wares.

At this time of year there were hardly any tourists – which suited Beth just fine. She preferred it when there were less people around. She liked to wander through the quaint old streets of shingled and clapboard houses and daydream about what it must have been like two hundred years ago when Sea Captain Moses Tucker bought the plot of land and built the house in which she now lived.

All in all, Beth thought as she sauntered toward Frenchies cafe for a spot of brunch, *my life would be just about perfect if I didn't have freckles and if I wasn't quite so skinny, and if Hal was less of a . . .*

She was almost knocked off her feet by Joe Moon, Hal's good-looking teenage brother. He stepped out of a hardware store with a cardboard box in his arms and cannoned right into her.

Beth went bright red. She didn't know why, but being near Joe always made her feel kind of squirmy and embarrassed.

'Hi, Joe,' she said, trying to look cool and sophisticated. 'Fancy bumping into you.' She gave a shrill, strangulated cackle of laughter. He just stared at her.

'Hi,' he said blankly.

'What's in the box?' *Keep him talking. Prove you're not some dumb, gawky kid.*

'Spares,' Joe said. Beth peered into the box. It was full of engine parts. Joe had been trying to fix his motorbike for the past nine months. Beth secretly hoped she'd get to be taken for a ride on it once it was all back in one piece again. Beth just loved motorbikes.

'Oh, right. Hey, will your bike be back on the road soon? Only I was wondering if—'

'I have a message for you,' Joe interrupted. 'Hal said to tell you something if I saw you.'

Beth's eyes narrowed. 'Oh, yeah? And what might that be?'

'He just said to say, *it's true.*' Joe shrugged and wandered off mumbling something that sounded like, 'Dumb kid games!'

Beth caught sight of herself in the storefront window. Her face was still red. Why did that have to happen to her every time she met up with Joe? It was so annoying.

Hal's final message for her had been left at Frenchies. He'd written it up on the menu board in green chalk.

BETH! IT'S TRUE! CALL ME! HAL!

She grabbed a cloth and wiped the message before ordering French toast with maple syrup and chopped walnuts.

She had to admit one thing about Hal: he didn't quit easily!

Beth lay on her bed that night, fully dressed, wide-eyed and watching the window. She had a really strong feeling that Hal was going to pull one of his stunts again during the night. If so much as a glimmer of green light showed through the blind, she was ready to dash downstairs and catch Hal in the act.

The digital display on her bedside clock showed ten past midnight. She yawned and settled herself more comfortably against the pillows.

She woke suddenly. It was seventeen minutes past one. She'd fallen asleep. There was no green light and no spooky noises. Maybe Hal wasn't planning on trying to fool her again that night after all.

Rubbing the sleep out of her eyes, she clambered off her bed and padded over to the window. She lifted a corner of the blind and squinted out into the night.

It was pitch dark out there. No stars. Nothing. It was like looking into a black hole.

Then the light flickered. A pale, wavering greenish light that seemed to hover insubstantially right in front of Beth's eyes, as if it was hanging in the air just outside her window.

She knuckled her eyes and looked again. Now she was able to get some kind of perspective on the light. It wasn't close by at all. In fact, it seemed like it was way out on the water. But it wasn't the kind of light used by ships. It was more of a wavering *glow*, as if a green light was being shone on to something out there.

'I knew it,' Beth whispered. She guessed that the absolute darkness of the night must be playing tricks on her eyes. The light couldn't actually be out in the sea; it had to be on the beach. Hal had set something up down there and now he was probably hidden away somewhere waiting for her to take the bait.

'OK, *Harrison*,' she mumured, using his hated full name, 'I'll bite! Let's see what tricks you've come up with. Let's go visit with some *aliens*.'

Beth slipped into a jacket and tiptoed down the stairs. She didn't want to risk waking anyone. Her mom was the kind of person who wouldn't take too kindly to knowing her daughter was out prowling the sea-front in the middle of the night. Even if Beth's purpose was only to beat the living daylights out of Hal the moment she set eyes on him.

She grabbed the flashlight that hung inside the basement door. The kitchen floor creaked as she headed for the back door. If the old house had been *trying* to let everyone know she was up and about, it couldn't have done a better job!

She stepped out into the cold, breezy night. The slap of chilly sea air took her by surprise and she pulled her jacket tighter around herself as she set off across the deck and down into the long grass.

A white stone wall marked the boundary of their back yard. Beth didn't switch the flashlight on. She was hoping to take Hal by surprise. She wanted to discover wherever he was hiding, sneak up behind him, and be all over him like a rash before he knew what had hit him.

Of course, there was always the chance that Hal had simply set the stunt up and then gone back home. But Beth was convinced he'd be around somewhere. After all, what's the point of a practical joke if you're not there to see whether it's worked or not?

Not for the first time, Beth was struck by how *black* the night was out here. She'd been brought up in New York, where it was never completely dark. There were always neon signs and streetlights to break up the darkness. But out here in Monasaukee Bay, a person could wave their hand right in front of their face and still have trouble figuring how many fingers they were holding up.

Beth climbed the wall and jumped down on to the narrow beach road. On the other side of the road was a strip of wild heather and spiky bushes that sloped down to the smooth sand. Scrub pine hid Hal's 'alien' light from view right then.

She crept across the road and into the scrubland,

keeping low and moving as quietly as possible. She took a long, elaborate zig-zag course through the scrub, hoping at any moment to catch Hal in his hiding place. In her imagination she saw herself beaning him with the rubber torch and then bouncing up and down on his stomach until he yelled for mercy.

But she came out on to the smooth slope of sand without any sight of him. And now she could see something that made her wonder what the *heck* was going on.

The green light wasn't on the beach at all. It really *was* way out on the water. Beth's eyes had gotten used to the darkness now, and she could make out the difference between the shapes and shadows of things around her.

She could just make out the long, low hump of Cranberry Island against the sky, and she could tell the sea from the clouded sky. The strange light was flickering and billowing out there like a candle in a strong wind, or like green fire.

Beth straightened up. She was totally baffled now. How could Hal have set this up? It wasn't like he had a row boat he could have taken out there. Even in the darkness, Beth could figure that the light had to be a good distance off-shore.

An amazing thought slid into her head, like a trickle of icy water.

BETH! IT'S TRUE! CALL ME! HAL!

Could Hal have been telling the truth? Had he *really* seen this light the previous night, and did he *truly* not know what the light was?

Beth walked down into the slow, steady lap of the sea-line. Cold water bubbled around her shoes as she strained her eyes into the night.

'Elizabeth Hunter, you're a total fool!' Beth hissed to herself. 'Why didn't you bring binoculars?'

The mystery of the ghostly green light wasn't to be unravelled by the naked eye. If Beth was going to be able to make any sense of it at all, she'd have to go back to the house and fetch some binoculars.

Beth began to backtrack up the beach, walking backwards as if the light had hypnotized her and she couldn't look away. What could it *be*?

Beth's mystery antennae were twitching like crazy. It sure didn't look like anything a person would expect to see out in the bay. If it was a boat, then it was the weirdest-lit boat Beth had ever seen. And if it *wasn't* a boat, then what on earth was it?

Giant, mutant, radioactive octopus-things!

Get out of here! Are you crazy?

Beth turned away from the shivering green light and made her way back through the bushes.

Then she heard it! A small sound. A crack or creak or something like that, away over to her right. The kind of noise a person might make when they were trying really hard to be quiet.

Beth dropped into an alert crouch. Hal! It had to be Hal! All her confusion drained away as Beth made her stealthy way toward the source of the tell-tale sound. It was Hal all along, just like she should have realised. She didn't know how he'd fixed it, but that darned light out there was definitely, positively, absolutely down to Hal Moon.

She saw his feet first, sticking out from behind a big, dark cranberry bush. He was lying there on the ground, probably waiting to see her come high-tailing it up the beach, shrieking about alien invaders.

Was *he* in for a surprise!

Beth crept around back of the bush. She didn't want him to know she was there until it was too late for him to be able to escape. She tiptoed nearer and nearer. She could see his legs now, but the top half of him was still hidden by the foliage.

She took a deep breath, gathered herself and pounced.

'Got you!' she hollered as she came crashing down on top of him. 'I'll teach you to play games with me!'

She realized her mistake in a second. The person lying on the ground behind the cranberry bush was Hal's size, but they were wearing some kind of loose grey overalls and their head was covered by a hood. And the reaction of that person to being suddenly jumped on was instantaneous and absolutely terrifying.

The body twisted under her and gave an almighty heave, sending the startled Beth flying through the air like a rag doll. And the next thing Beth knew, she was flat on her back with a heavy weight pressing down on her chest and two long-fingered hands clutched at her throat as though with the intention of choking the life out of her.

5

The strength and power of her attacker left Beth stunned and gasping for breath. Her long hair was covering her face and she could only catch the vaguest glimpse of the person holding her down. A white, wedge-shaped face loomed above her, the eyes hidden in pools of black shadow.

She snatched for the hands that clutched at her throat. Her fingers closed around twig-thin wrists.

'Stop it! Stop it!' Beth yelled as she fought to prize the hands away. 'Are you crazy? You're *hurting* me!'

It was like a nightmare. Her attacker didn't make a sound. The night reeled around, rimmed with red fire as the pressure increased on her neck.

And then, suddenly, as if from far away and from a whole other world, she heard Hal's voice. Shouting.

Instantly the fingers relaxed at her throat and the weight lifted from her chest. She rolled on to her side, coughing and spluttering. Through the thick obscuring veils of her hair, she saw a slight, grey figure dart away through the stunted pine bushes.

Moments later someone came crashing down in the trampled heather at her side.

'Beth? Are you OK?'

Beth sat up. She yanked the tangled curls of her thick hair off her face and stared into Hal's anxious eyes.

'Are you OK?' he asked again.

'I – I think so,' she gasped dizzily. And then her brain got back into gear. 'Heck, no!' she said. 'No, I'm not OK at all! Some sicko crazy person just tried to strangle me.'

She whipped her head around but it was too late. Her attacker had been swallowed up by the night.

'Did you see him?' she asked Hal. 'Did you get a good look at him?'

'Not really,' Hal said. 'I heard you yelling and I came running. All I saw was his back as he ran off. He was wearing some sort of grey clothes with a hood up over his head.'

Beth rubbed her neck. It was a little sore, but fortunately Hal had arrived before any damage had been done. Beth preferred not to think what might have happened if Hal *hadn't* arrived at exactly the right moment. It was just the way the good guys always turned up in the nick of time in a movie.

'Who was it, Beth?' Hal asked.

She looked at him. 'He didn't exactly introduce himself,' she croaked. 'I can't believe how strong he was. I mean, he was really skinny and small, but he threw me through the air like I was *nothing*.'

'But what happened? Did he just attack you out of nowhere or what?'

'Well, I guess you could say I attacked him,' Beth admitted. 'I thought he was *you*.'

Hal blinked at her. 'You attacked him because you thought he was me?' he said slowly.

'That's right,' Beth said. 'I came down here to find out what the deal was with that green light you set up. And I saw the guy hiding, and I thought it was you, so naturally I jumped on him.'

'Naturally,' Hal said dryly. 'But—'

'Except that it wasn't you,' Beth interrupted. 'It was some *other* geek with a really weird face.'

'A weird face?' Hal said. 'What do you mean?'

'My hair was in my eyes, so I didn't get much of a look at him,' Beth said. 'But he had totally *white* skin and these huge great black *eyes*.'

'Maybe he was wearing sunglasses?' Hal suggested.

'Get real,' Beth said. 'What sort of person would wear sunglasses in the middle of the night?'

'Well, excuse me,' Hal said, 'but what sort of person would be out here in the middle of the night *at all*?'

'Beats me,' Beth said. She was beginning to recover now. She stood up, brushing dirt and bits of twig off her clothes. 'I guess if *I* was jumped on in the night, I'd get pretty mad. The thing I can't get over is how strong he was for such a skinny little guy. I mean, he can't have been much taller than me but once he was on top of me I couldn't *move*.'

'Are you going to report it?' Hal asked.

'Well, let's think this over,' Beth said. 'Hey, mom, call the cops, I've just been half strangled by some little guy that I bushwhacked while I was creeping about out on the beach in the middle of the night.' She gave Hal a hooded look. 'Does that sound like the kind of thing you'd tell your folks?'

Hal gave a soft laugh. 'I guess not,' he said.

'Me neither,' Beth said. She looked thoughtfully into Hal's face.

'What?' he asked.

'You came along at just the right time,' she said. 'Thanks for frightening that guy off.'

Hal shrugged. 'It was nothing,' he said.

'Really? Oh, well, forget I mentioned it, then.'

'No, wait up,' Hal said. 'I didn't mean it was *nothing at all*. I mean, I saved you, didn't I? It was a really heroic thing to have done. When I said it was *nothing*, I was, kind of saying there was no need to make a big fuss about it. I was just the right guy in the right place at the right time.'

Beth patted him on the shoulder. 'They'll make a movie of it one day,' she said. 'In the meantime you can 'fess up on how you fixed that green light-thing out there.'

'I didn't.'

'Excuse me?'

'I didn't set up that light out there,' Hal said vehemently. 'It wasn't me. Honest, truly, hope-to-be-staked-out-in-Death-Valley-and-eaten-by-buzzards, I didn't do it.'

'So, if it's nothing to do with you,' Beth said suspiciously, 'what the heck were you doing wandering about out here at this time of night, huh? Answer me that!'

'Investigating,' Hal said. 'Collecting evidence. Look.'

Beth had been too busy with other things to have noticed that Hal had a small case hanging from a strap around his neck. He opened the case and pulled out an expensive-looking camera and a pair of binoculars.

Beth gazed at the things in his hands and then looked searchingly into his face.

'Are you on the level about this?' she asked. 'Because I'm telling you right now, Harrison Moon, if this is just another of your meat-head jokes I'm never, ever going to forgive you for as long as I live.'

Hal looked solemnly at her. 'Look, Beth, if I'm not telling the truth, may I be struck by a bolt of lightning and burned to a crisp.'

'OK,' Beth said. 'I believe you.' She looked over her shoulder toward the sea. 'Can you *take* pictures of stuff in the dark?'

'Not with a regular camera,' Hal said. 'But this is a special kind of camera, see? It's my dad's. You can vary the shutter speed. You can slow it right down so you can take pictures at night.'

'So, let's go take some pictures.'

Hal grinned at her and patted the camera. 'They're already in here,' he said. 'I've taken a whole film full. I was on my way back home when I heard you yelling. I think we're going to see some pretty amazing stuff when we get the pictures enlarged. Even better than the stuff I saw through the binoculars.'

'What did you see?'

'A couple of things,' Hal said. 'Something that might have been a person, down by the water's edge. And . . .' His voice faded.

'Yes? And *what*?'

'Well, it was kind of hazy,' Hal admitted. 'But I'm pretty much sure that I saw something moving about out there. A moving shape in the light.'

'A shape?' Beth breathed. 'What kind of shape?'

'A human shape,' Hal said. 'But kind of strange. Too big for a regular person. I don't mean too tall, I mean too bulky. I know what it reminded me of, Beth.'

'Uh-huh?'

'It looked just like someone in a spacesuit.'

'Hal!'

'I know, I know!' Hal said. 'You don't have to *tell* me it's crazy. I'm just saying what it looked like, that's all.'

'You know something,' Beth said. 'You have some nerve, doing all this stuff without me.'

'What-at?' Hal gasped. 'Didn't I try to tell you

about the weird light? And didn't I leave a whole load of messages for you to call me?'

'Well, excuse me, but that's not the point at all,' Beth said. 'If a person didn't have such a reputation for playing dumb tricks on another person, then maybe a person might be trusted just a little more.' Beth stretched out a hand. 'Now, gimme those binoculars, I want to see that guy in the *spacesuit*.'

Hal handed her the binoculars and followed her as she marched back down to the sand.

'I never said I thought it *was* a spacesuit,' he mumbled under his breath. 'I just said it *looked* like a spacesuit.'

Beth stopped suddenly.

'Rats!' she said. 'Rats, rats, and more rats!'

Hal looked over her shoulder. The reason for her exclamation was obvious at a glance. The freaky green light was gone. The ocean was featureless and black and as empty as a piece torn out of the world.

As if to make her disappointment more acute, a finger of cold air searched its way in under Beth's jacket and made her shiver. Suddenly, as if all the strangeness and danger and excitement of the night had come together like a fog in her head, Beth felt totally exhausted.

She turned and looked at Hal.

'Here's the thing,' she said, suppressing a yawn with the back of her hand. 'You and I are going down to the drugstore *first thing* tomorrow morning with that film. And we'll have some enlargements made, like you said.'

'Yeah,' Hal said. 'And then what?'

'Well, whatever is going on out there,' Beth said, 'I figure it isn't your every-day, average, ordinary boat-trip-to-Cranberry-Island-type-thing, OK?'

'No way!'

'So, once we have the pictures, we go to the police and tell them everything,' Beth said. '*And* we'll have the pictures to prove it.' She yawned again. 'But right now, all I want to do is hit the hay. This has been *some* night.'

They walked side by side up the beach.

'In the meantime,' Hal said, 'we could come up with a few theories of our own about the light, huh? Like, it could be a *ghost ship*.' He lowered his voice to a husky whisper. 'A ship of the dead, doomed forever to sail the oceans of the world in penance of some terrible crime. Hey – what about a *pirate* ghost ship, huh?'

'Yeah, sure,' Beth said sleepily. 'Ghost pirates in spacesuits. The police will really eat up *that* theory, Hal.'

Beth and Hal parted company on the beach road. Beth clambered wearily over the wall and plodded up the garden. A couple of minutes later she tumbled into bed and fell asleep, like a diver plunging into deep water.

But it was an uneasy sleep, filled with disturbing dreams of flickering green lights and pale faces with huge black eyes; and clutching skeletal hands with long, crooked, bony fingers.

6

Beth was up with the lark the following morning. She pulled up the blind and gazed out over the familiar panorama of Monasaukee Bay. A light dusting of mist made the pale orange sun look like it was dissolving into the air.

It was as if all the weirdness and danger of the previous night had been swept clean away, like sandwriting obliterated by a rising tide.

'Ghost pirates in spacesuits,' Beth chuckled to herself as she got dressed. 'As *if*!' In the cool light of morning, it felt like there would be a perfectly rational explanation for everything.

Still, that green light *did* need some investigating. Beth was far too inquisitive to let a mystery like that go unsolved.

She waded through the dew-laden grass and headed across to Hal's house. Mrs Moon was wandering along the road with a big, beaming smile on her face and her arms full of brown and gold and yellow and deep-red leaves.

'Hello,' Beth said. 'It's a lovely morning.'

'It sure is,' Mrs Moon said in a vague, faraway voice. 'I love this time of year. I always collect some fallen leaves. They're such gorgeous colours to have around the house.' Hal's mother was an artist. Beth figured that was why she acted a little *odd* at times.

'Uh, are you heading back to the house?' Beth asked. 'I've come to see Hal.'

Mrs Moon nodded and Beth walked with her along the path and up the wooden steps to the front door.

Beth was used to having the run of the Moons' house. She trotted up the stairs. If things were going as normal, she'd have to drag Hal out of his bed. That guy would sleep all day if he was allowed to.

But Hal wasn't in bed. He wasn't even in his room. Beth came out into the hallway and heard the sound of the shower running in the nearby bathroom.

'It's a miracle,' Beth murmured to herself as she went back into Hal's room to wait. 'It's still only morning, and Hal Moon is up and about.'

She yawned and sat on his bed. Nosily, she started looking through the stuff on his bedside table to pass the time.

The black and silver spine of a large hardback

book caught her eye and she slid it out from under a bunch of comics and magazines.

Her heart skipped a beat as she saw the picture on the front cover of the book. She rested it across her knees and stared dazedly down at it, her stomach churning and the hairs at the back of her neck prickling and sparking.

She couldn't believe what she was looking at. It was crazy. It wasn't possible.

'Hiya, Beth,' Hal said as she came into the room, fully dressed but with wet hair and a towel over his shoulder. 'Make yourself at home, why don't you?'

Beth ignored his mild attempt at sarcasm. She lifted the book in both hands.

'What's this?' she asked in a dry, husky voice.

'Hmm, *difficult*,' Hal said, towelling his wet hair. 'Uh, could it be a *book*?'

Beth turned the book so Hal could look at the front cover.

The cover was black with silver writing. *The Darkwood Incident; An Investigation Into Alien Encounters*. Beneath the writing was an illustration: a pale, unearthly triangular face stared out with huge, black almond-shaped eyes.

'It's the guy from last night,' Beth croaked, the book shaking in her hands.

Hal let out a peal of laughter. 'Good joke, Beth!'
Beth glared at him. 'I'm not joking.'

'Sure, you're not,' Hal said with a grin.

'*HAL!*' Beth shrieked. 'I'm not *kidding*! You think
I'm kidding? Look at me – I'm shaking like a leaf.
What the heck is this book all about, Hal? Who is
this guy supposed to be?'

'It's just a drawing,' Hal said. 'An artist's
impression of what some people thought they
saw around here a few years back. Darkwood
is a tiny little town a few miles from here.
The film my dad is working on right now was
inspired by the book. Some people said they were
abducted by aliens. It's all hogwash.' Hal nodded
knowledgeably. 'Trust me, it was all some kind
of mass hysteria. They'd probably been eating
magic mushrooms or something. But it made for
a cute story.'

'You're not listening to me,' Beth hissed urgently.
'I told you that the guy last night had a weird face.'
Beth shook the book. 'He looked *exactly* like this
picture, Hal.'

'You're crazy,' Hal said dismissively. 'You said
you hardly saw him, and all of a sudden you're
totally convinced he was an alien? Get real, Beth!
I know you have a real wild imagination, but this
is *way* out of line, even for you.'

Beth didn't say another word. She put the book down, stood up and marched out of his room.

'Hey, Beth!'

'Just give me a minute!' Beth snapped.

'But—'

She walked into the bathroom, leaving the door wide open. Puzzled, Hal followed her. Beth leaned into the shower booth and twisted the dial. A gush of cold water cascaded down over her head.

'Beth!'

She let the cold water run over her lowered head for a minute or two before blindly groping to turn the flood off.

'Beth Hunter, you are *insane*,' Hal said as she straightened up and turned to face him. Water flowed off the saturated mass of her long red hair and dripped down her face.

'I needed to clear my head,' Beth spluttered. She grabbed a towel and stalked back into Hal's room.

'OK,' she said, pacing up and down in front of the window, and rubbing her hair with the towel. 'This is a multiple choice question, right? One: I saw an alien. Two: I saw some guy who just happened to look like an alien. Three: I imagined the whole thing.'

'I'm not saying you *imagined* it,' Hal said. 'For sure you didn't imagine it. I mean, I saw the little guy, too. But there's no way he was an alien. He was just some *guy*.'

'Is there a description in that book of what the aliens were like?' Beth asked.

'Sure, plenty of them.'

'Read some out to me.'

Hal picked up the book and riffled through the pages. Beth paced silently up and down as Hal read out four or five descriptions of what the people of Darkwood thought they had seen.

'So,' Beth said. 'Basically, everyone said the aliens were short and thin, but very strong. And they wore grey clothes or had grey skin; and they had triangular faces and great big black eyes.'

'Yup,' Hal said. 'Pretty much your standard alien dude. Except that it's all *hooey*. I mean, no way have aliens landed on this planet.'

'How come you're so sure about that?'

'Because the nearest inhabitable planet would have to be millions and millions and *millions* of miles away,' Hal said. 'If a bunch of aliens *did* bother to travel all that way it would take hundreds of years and use up huge amounts of fuel. And do you really think, after all that *effort*, that they'd wind up wandering about in a nowhere place like Darkwood?'

'They might have crashed,' Beth said. 'And anyway, you don't *know* it would take them hundreds of years. Maybe they have warp drive so they can travel faster than the speed of light.'

'Of course they don't!'

'Why the heck not?'

'Because there's no such thing as warp drive, you total basket-case,' Hal exclaimed. 'It's just a made-up science fiction thing. It's impossible to travel faster than light.'

'Oh, right,' Beth said. 'Like, *you* know everything. Listen! *We* might not have warp drive, Hal Smarty-pants Moon, but *they* might have.'

Hal ran to the door and leaned out into the hallway.

'Go fetch the men in the white coats!' he hollered. 'Beth has finally flipped!'

'OK, OK,' Beth shouted. 'So you think I'm crazy. Well, *fine*! Thanks for the vote of confidence. I come up with some logical explanation for what went on last night, and all you can do is make fun!'

'What *logical* explanation?' Hal asked.

'OK, here's the thing,' Beth said. 'This alien guy was zipping around in his spaceship, taking notes and stuff, when – phut! phutter! phuuuu-glurk! Something goes wrong with the motor.' Hal watched as Beth went into an elaborate pantomime of the alien wrestling with his controls. 'He's gonna crash! But he doesn't want to risk being discovered, so he belly-flops the ship out in the ocean. Ker-splash!'

Hal gazed at her as if she was insane. 'Yup,' he said. 'I'm with you so far.'

'The spaceship catches fire,' Beth continued. 'It bursts into *green* flames, right?'

'Uh-huh.'

'The alien guy jumps overboard and swims for the shore. His spaceship is, like, totally burning up. He collapses in a heap on the beach, completely exhausted. And then I come along and disturb him. Which is why he attacked me. He didn't want any earth-people catching sight of him, right? Then you arrive and he runs off.'

'And the space-ship?' Hal asked mildly.

'I guess it sank,' Beth concluded. She gave Hal a long, slow look. 'Well, at least it beats your ghost-pirates-in-spacesuits theory.'

'Yeah, except that wasn't a *theory*, Beth. That was a *joke*. I can't believe you're serious about this, man. It's crazy to the max!'

Beth folded her arms. 'So, let's hear what you think we saw last night.'

'I'll tell you what I think,' Hal said. 'I think we saw something that was supposed to be a big secret. Maybe it was some super-secret experiment that went wrong. That would explain that guy I saw out there in the big suit. I've been thinking about it. My guess is that he was wearing some sort of protective clothing, like fire fighters do, you know? I think something exploded or leaked out and caught fire on board a boat, and that guy was trying to control the incident. And once he had the fire under control, he got out of there just as quick as he could. And maybe that guy you jumped on was keeping watch for him. You didn't see big black eyes, Beth, what you saw was some protective goggles.'

Beth looked at the book, lying face-up on Hal's bed. Then she looked at Hal.

'What *kind* of super-secret experiment?' she asked slowly.

'Beats me,' Hal said. 'How about we go get the film processed? I bet those pictures will give us some real clues.'

Beth sighed. 'I totally hate you,' she said.

'Why?'

'Because that's probably more-or-less what

61

happened,' Beth said miserably. 'And I *really* wanted it to be aliens. Come on, let's go hand the film over. And you can buy me a blueberry muffin as a punishment.'

'A punishment for what?' Hal asked as he chased her down the stairs.

'For being *right*!'

7

'It's a raw kind of a day to go swimming, people.' Mr Kowalski looked at Hal and Beth from behind the counter in the drugstore. He finished writing the receipt for their film and handed it to them.

'We haven't been swimming,' Beth said, puzzled by the comment.

'Oh, the wet hair,' Hal said, realizing why the storekeeper thought they must have just come back from a quick dip in the bay. Both of them still had wet hair, and Beth had wet patches down her clothes. 'It's the latest hair style, Mr Kowalski. Everyone is doing it in New York. It's called the *wet look*.'

'You don't say?' Mr Kowalski said. 'What will they think of next, huh?' He shook his head and then shrugged, as though trendy New York hair styles were something beyond his understanding. 'Your pictures will be ready in about an hour.'

They walked out into the street.

Beth looked at Hal.

'What?' he said innocently.

'You can't help it, can you?' she said. 'You have to make with the jokes all the time.'

Hal smiled. 'So, what do we do for the next hour? Go sit in Frenchies?'

'I've had a thought,' Beth said. 'We want to investigate that green light properly, right? I mean, like, *professionally*.'

'Check.'

'When the police investigate things,' Beth continued, 'they send a team out to ask people questions. You know, to find out if there are any witnesses around. I think we should do that.'

'What? Send a team out?'

'No, dummy. Ask questions,' Beth said. 'Maybe someone else saw the light out there.'

'Yeah, or maybe someone will actually know what it was,' Hal said. 'That's a good idea, Beth. It'll save us making total fools of ourselves if we find out in advance that it was something completely ordinary and normal, like . . . uh . . . um . . .'

'Yeah? Go on,' Beth said. 'Like *what*, exactly?'

'Like an experimental light-rig for night fishing,' Hal said. 'Special green light to attract the fish.'

Beth looked at him. 'Heck, I really hope it isn't

something like that. That would be so *boring* it's not true!'

'So, let's go ask some questions. The guys down at the quay will be able to tell us if it's anything to do with fishing.'

They walked down the gently sloping road to The Front. The slightly run-down quay area was over to the right. Years ago, New Greenwich had been a thriving fishing port, but nowadays the old fishing boats were only used for tourist trips around the bay or were chartered in the summer by bunches of city people to go sea-fishing with poles and buckets of live bait.

The few boat owners who still made a living off the tourists spent the off-season months refurbishing their boats and drinking in The Whaler bar or just sitting around playing checkers or poker.

Beth liked the slightly rascally atmosphere that surrounded the boat-men. She liked the thick sweaters and heavy boots and the sharp, briney smell that hung around them. And she liked the way their eyes always seemed to be searching for something that lay hidden just beyond the horizon.

Beth and Hal were hit by the strong smell of varnish and paint as they stepped out on to the boardwalk and made their way along to the big, solitary, shabby black hut known as The Whaler.

Tables and benches filled the forecourt, over-looking the bay. The early mist had lifted and Cranberry Island could clearly be seen across the choppy water, long, and very low and patterned with patches of heather and cranberry bushes and scrub pine.

Most of the men were busy fixing their boats up after the hectic summer season, but a few were sitting outside the bar.

'I think we should decide what kind of questions to ask,' Hal said softly. 'Because, if we just—' But Beth was gone. She strode out on to the forecourt of the bar like she owned the place.

'Hi,' Beth said as she approached the nearest table. 'Did any of you see anything strange out in the bay last night?' she asked the four men seated at the table.

So much for the subtle approach, Hal thought as he followed her.

No one at that table seemed to have seen anything. Beth moved on to the next one. Her question was answered by a puzzled shake of heads.

After four unsuccessful tries, she came to a table near the entrance to the bar. Two men were sitting there. One was quite young, unshaven and sullen-eyed, the other broad-beamed and grizzled, like an old bear.

'Hello, there, lassie,' said the older man. His keen grey eyes were enlivened by laughter-lines. 'If you want a trip around the bay, it'll cost you twenty five dollars, and that's cutting my own throat.'

Beth smiled. 'No, thanks,' she said. 'I'm *investigating*.' Beth suddenly wished she'd thought to bring a notebook. *Darn! That would have looked so much more professional!*

'Is that a fact?' said the man. 'And what might you be investigating, young lady?'

'Well, here's the thing,' Beth began. 'I was wondering if either of you saw anything, uh, *unusual* out in the bay last night.'

'Well, now you mention it, I did see something,' the older man said.

Hal noticed the black-haired younger man give him a sharp, almost *dangerous* look.

'You did?' Beth said. 'Like, what?'

'There was a whole troop of pink elephants dancing the tango out on Cranberry Island,' the older man said. 'About midnight, that would have been.' The man's eyes twinkled with mischief. 'Of course, I'd spent the evening in The Whaler, so

I could be wrong.' He laughed a loud, throaty laugh.

Hal saw the younger man relax a little and grin at the joke. He jerked a thumb at his companion.

'Archie sees all kinds of things after a night in The Whaler,' the young man said in a deep, rasping voice. 'He likes his beer.'

Beth frowned. 'Well, honestly!' she said. 'I'm trying to be *serious*. Did you *really* see anything strange?'

'What kind of strange?' Archie asked.

'Green light,' Beth said. 'Out near Cranberry Island.'

'Saint Elmo's fire,' the younger man said. 'That's what you saw.'

'Saint Elmo's fire?' Beth repeated. 'What's that?'

'It's a ghostly green light, like cold flames,' the young man said in a sepulchral voice. 'It's caused by electricity building up in the air. It catches hold of anything that sticks up into it. Like the mast of a ship, for instance. It can run down a mast and light up a whole ship.' He grinned. 'It can be kind of spooky if you don't know what it is, but it don't do no harm.'

'Oh.' Beth felt quite stunned by this. Saint Elmo's fire? Could that green light really have just been some kind of weird natural phenomenon all along?

Hal stepped up behind her. 'I didn't think Saint Elmo's fire occurred this far north,' he said. 'I thought I read that it happened more in the southern hemisphere.'

'You can't believe everything you read, boy,' the younger man said. Hal saw Archie looking at the younger man with a curious expression on his face, as if he had something on his mind that he didn't want to say out loud.

'I'll get some beer,' Archie said. He got up and walked slowly across the dark wooden planking of the forecourt and into the bar.

Beth glanced at Hal. 'Are you saying it *can't* have been Saint Elbow's fire?'

'Saint *Elmo's*.'

'Whatever! Answer the question.'

'I'm not saying it's impossible,' Hal said. 'But the article I read definitely said—'

The low growl of the younger man interrupted him.

'There's an old sailors' belief,' he said, staring hard at Hal with his brooding, black eyes, 'that a person who sees Saint Elmo's fire from dry land should never talk about it.'

'Really?' Beth said. 'Why ever not?'

'It's bad luck,' said the man. 'Real bad luck.'

'Is that so?' Beth said with deep scepticism. She grinned around at Hal. 'Hey, you'd better throw those pictures away, Hal, or something terrible might happen to you.'

'Pictures?' the man snapped. 'You took pictures?'

'We sure did,' Hal said. 'A whole reel full. We're having then developed right now.' He looked at Beth. 'I wonder if The Clarion would be interested in printing one? They might even *pay* me.'

'Us, you mean.'

'I took the pictures.'

'Are we a team, or what?'

'OK: *us*. But, if — oh!' During their brief exchange, the young man had gotten up from the table and was walking rapidly away along the quay, as if he'd suddenly remembered something urgent that he had to do.

'Thanks for your help,' Beth called after him.

'There's something funny about that guy,' Hal said.

'Yeah? He didn't make me laugh.'

'Not that kind of funny.' Hal glanced cautiously around. Archie was on his way back from the bar with two glasses of beer.

'Hey, now,' he said, 'where's Drew gone?'

Beth pointed. The young man was trotting

across the road. As they watched he vanished up a side street.

Archie sat down. 'I guess he'll be back.'

Hal looked at him. 'Do you think what we saw could have been Saint Elmo's fire?' he asked. 'This far north?'

'The oceans of this world are full of strange things,' Archie said, scratching his chin with stubby, work-worn fingers. 'Take squids, now. I was diving one time, down in Tamarind Bay, and I saw a squid *hypnotise* a ten foot barracuda by changing the colour of its body like it was some kind of living strobe light. Ate that old barracuda alive, he did, and the barracuda never moved a muscle.' He looked at the two friends. 'When a man's seen something like that, he doesn't say nothing's impossible. It could have been the fire, OK. Seems like the only explanation, don't it?'

'Well, actually I do have another theory—' Beth began.

'We'd better be going,' Hal said, grabbing Beth by the arm and towing her away. 'Bye.'

Beth dug her heels in half-way down the boardwalk.

'Aren't we going to ask any more questions?' she said, shaking Hal's hand off her arm.

71

'For someone who thinks she's a really great detective, you sure don't *see* much,' Hal said.

'What are you talking about?'

'Didn't you see the way Drew looked at Archie when Archie said he'd seen something last night?' Hal said. 'He looked at him like he was afraid Archie was going to give something away. And I'll tell you something else: no way was that Saint Elmo's fire out there last night. The atmospheric conditions are all wrong for it to happen this far north.'

'So the guy was wrong,' Beth said. 'Big deal.'

'You still don't get it, do you?' Hal said patiently. 'He wasn't *wrong*. He told us it was Saint Elmo's fire because that's what he wanted *us* to believe. I'll bet you anything you like that he *knows* what the green light was, and he was trying to throw us off the scent with that garbage about Saint Elmo's fire. And when I didn't buy it, he came up with that cornball story about it being bad luck to talk about it.'

'Yeah, but—'

'Beth! For once in your life just trust me on this. That Drew guy *knows* something. And it's something he doesn't want us to know.'

'So why are we standing here *talking*?' Beth demanded. 'We should be following him.'

'I was trying to,' Hal said. 'You're the one who insisted on stopping.'

'Huh!' Beth exclaimed. 'Any excuse! Come on, let's go!'

Hal opened his mouth to say something, but closed it again without speaking. Beth was already half way across the road, running toward the side street up which Drew had disappeared.

With a helpless shake of his head, Hal chased after her. Sometimes, life with Beth was really hard work!

8

'Where do you think he went?' Beth stood panting a little at the top end of the long, sloping side street. There was no sign of Drew.

Hal leaned against a wall and caught his breath. 'You'll have to give me a minute to get my psychic powers on-line, Beth,' he said with deep sarcasm. 'For heaven's sake, how should I know where he went? Maybe he suddenly realized he'd left the gas burning on the stove.'

Beth ignored Hal's comment. 'What say we hunt around for a while?' she suggested. 'I mean, it's not like this is such a huge place that a person can just disappear. We're bound to find him sooner or later.'

'Fine,' Hal said. 'Let's split up. That'll give us twice the chance of finding the guy. We'll meet back at Frenchies in, say,' he looked at his watch, 'half an hour, OK?'

'Yup,' Beth said with a nod. 'And make sure he doesn't see you, OK? We wanna know what made him run off like that and we don't want him to know he's being followed, right?'

Hal frowned at her. 'Of course I won't let him see me,' he said. 'Sometimes you make like you think I'm a total idiot.'

Beth grinned. 'Only sometimes? I must be slipping.' She headed off to the right. 'See you at Frenchies,' she called back. 'In thirty minutes.'

When Hal arrived at Frenchies, it was to find Beth already sitting at their favourite window seat, munching her way through a choc chip muffin. A second muffin sat on the plate and she'd bought two chocolate milkshakes.

'Wuwwwl?' she mumbled through a mouthful of muffin as he sat down opposite her. 'Howwwowww woo?'

'Huh?'

Beth chewed and swallowed. 'How'd you do?'

Hal shook his head. 'Nix.'

'Yeah, me too,' Beth said. 'I guess we're going to have to be a little more scientific about this.' She looked thoughtfully at Hal. 'Are you absolutely one-hundred-per-cent certain that the guy was acting strange?'

Hal nodded. He explained again about the sharp look Drew had given Archie, and about his obvious relief that Archie was just telling a joke.

'And didn't you see the way Archie looked at Drew when he started talking about Saint Elmo's fire?' Hal continued persuasively. 'Archie knew he was talking hogwash.'

'So why didn't he just come out and say so?' Beth said.

'Exactly!' Hal exclaimed.

'What do you mean: *exactly*? Exactly what?'

Hal took a deep breath. 'Well,' he said, 'the way I see it, Drew knows something about the green light.' Hal lowered his voice a little as a man in a smart blue suit walked by and sat at the adjoining table. 'Drew knows what was going on out there, and Archie *knows* he knows. And I'll bet you two hundred squillion dollars that the thing that Drew knows, and which Archie knows he knows, is . . .' Hal stopped. 'I've lost track of what I was saying now,' he said.

'Archie knows what Drew knows,' Beth said helpfully. 'And Drew knows that Archie knows what he knows. But what I want to know, is what is it that Drew knows, and Archie knows, and Drew knows Archie knows and Archie knows Drew knows.'

'I don't know,' Hal said.

Beth dropped her head into her hands. 'A person could lose their mind talking to you, Harrison Moon!'

'Only if a person had a mind to lose in the first place, *Elizabeth*!' Hal retorted. 'Listen, if people know what the green light is, but won't admit it, that must mean my theory is right.'

'Which theory?'

'That there was something top secret going on out there,' Hal said.

'Excuse me, but just how *top secret* can a thing be if every low-life in town knows about it?' Beth said.

'You're missing out part two of the theory,' Hal said. He held a finger up. 'Someone is up to something secret out in the bay.' He lifted a second finger. 'Something went wrong. And it was something going wrong that caused the green light. Now, maybe a few people like Drew and Archie *saw* the light and went out in their boats to investigate. And maybe they were paid-off or told to keep their mouths shut about it. Maybe they were even told to use Saint Elmo's fire as a cover story in case anyone came around asking questions.' Hal rocked his chair back on two legs with a smug look on his face.

'They didn't reckon on tangling with *me*,' he said. 'I guess I was just too smart for them.'

Beth stretched out a foot under the table and gave Hal's chair a nudge. Hal's arms windmilled as he fought for balance and only just saved himself from landing in an undignified heap on the floor.

'Well?' he asked once he'd gotten himself level again. 'What do you say? Is that a great theory or what?'

Beth sucked up some of the thick shake and let her hand rock slowly in the air. 'So-so,' she said. 'I still like my crash-landed alien theory best.'

'I thought we dumped that way back,' Hal said.

'It's OK for you,' Beth remarked. 'You didn't get half strangled by the . . . *thing* . . . the *whatever-it-was* out there last night. I *saw* it up real close, and it definitely looked just like that drawing on the front cover of your alien encounters book.'

'Puh-leeeze!' Hal sighed. 'Enough with the aliens, already. I want to get to the bottom of this. I want to know what *really* went on out there.'

'So do I.'

'Well, in that case, what say we mosey on down to the drugstore and pick up my pictures? They should be ready by now, and if my guess is right, they're going to show us *exactly* what that green light was.'

The two friends finished their food and walked out of the cafe. Hal noticed that the man in the blue suit, who had been sitting there doing nothing more unusual than drinking coffee and reading a newspaper, got up as soon as they did and left the cafe only a few paces behind them.

Hal glanced over his shoulder as they made their way to Mr Kowalski's drugstore. The sharp blue suit was strolling along behind them. The man seemed kind of out of place to Hal.

'Don't look round,' Hal whispered to Beth, 'but I think we're being followed.'

Beth looked over her shoulder. The man in the blue suit was standing looking in a storefront window. He seemed oblivious to the two friends.

'What, him?' Beth said. 'No way. He's just some *guy*.'

'I don't *believe* you sometimes,' Hal hissed. 'I said *don't* look round.'

'Quit moaning,' Beth said as they crossed the road to the drugstore. 'Do you have the receipt?'

Hal pulled out the slip of paper as they walked into the drugstore. It only took Mr Kowalski a minute or two to get to them.

'I think there's something wrong with your camera, son,' Mr Kowalski said as he slid the envelope across the counter. 'Not one of your pictures has come out right. I think you need to go see a specialist and get it fixed before you waste any more films.'

Hal picked up the envelope and opened the flap. Beth breathed down his neck as he drew out the wad of shiny pictures. Black with a small greeny-white splodge in the middle. He turned to the second picture. It was the same.

'See what I mean, son?' Mr Kowalski said. 'You need to get that fixed.'

'Actually, these are exactly what I wanted,' Hal said. 'How long would it take you to print off some enlargements for me?'

'I could probably have them for you by Tuesday. What size do you want?'

Beth thumbed through the pictures while Hal and Mr Kowalski spoke.

All the pictures were the same except for one. Beth picked it out and brought it up close to her face to try and make something of the grey shapes that were caught in a blurry haze at the left hand edge.

Hal had been right: that shape *did* look like someone standing down by the water. In fact, the closer she looked, the more she was convinced it was *two* people – one slightly behind the other. Two frustratingly blurred figures that looked like they were wearing grey cover-alls. And one face seemed to be turned toward the camera: and the eyes were big black holes!

She stepped out of the store to examine the picture in full daylight.

'Wow!' she breathed.

'We'll be back in a while,' Hal said to Mr Kowalski,' I've just got to work out how many enlargements I can afford.' He followed Beth out of the store.

'Aren't we having the enlargements done?' she asked.

'Sure, we are,' Hal said. 'But we need to figure out which pictures to have blown up. Enlargements as big as we're going to need are pretty expensive. I can't afford to get more than two or three done. Let's go somewhere quiet and take a proper look through the pictures so we can decide.'

'I've already seen one picture that will be worth the cost,' Beth said. 'And you were wrong – there wasn't *one* person down by the sea – there were *two*! *If* they were *people* at all!'

'Show me,' Hal said.

Beth handed him the pictures.

'Wow! You're right!'

Someone suddenly walked right in front of them as they were about to cross the street.

Hal looked up in surprise. It was the man in the blue suit.

'Excuse me, young man, young lady,' he said in a smooth, refined voice. 'I wonder if I could take up a moment or two of your time?'

'Sure,' Beth said with a smile. 'What can we do for you?'

'Maybe we could go somewhere a little more private?' the man suggested.

Beth's eyes narrowed. 'I don't think we'll be doing that,' she said suspiciously. 'What do you want?'

'And maybe you'd like to tell us why you've been following us?' Hal added.

The man smiled suavely. 'You misunderstand,' he said, 'although I'm impressed by your caution. It certainly wouldn't be a good idea for you to go off with a stranger, but I only meant maybe we could take a seat over there?' He pointed to one of the wooden benches that lined the seafront. 'My name is Richard MacNamarra. I work for a specialist government bureau. Come on, you'll be interested in what I have to say, I can promise you.'

Beth and Hal looked at each other then shrugged.

'OK,' Beth said. 'I guess I can always scream for the police if you turn out to be a weirdo.'

They walked across the road and sat down on the bench, Hal and Beth together at one end and Richard MacNamarra at the other.

'The people I work for sent me here to do some investigating,' Richard MacNamarra said. Beth's mystery antennae pricked up immediately. An investigation! 'I work for a government organisation called the BPA.' He smiled. 'Maybe you've heard of us?'

'I don't think I have,' Beth said. 'What do the initials stand for?'

Richard MacNamarra leaned toward them and fixed them with his bright blue eyes.

'I'm a field agent,' he said conspiratorially, 'for the Bureau of Paranormal Affairs. I have reason to believe you may be able to help me with an investigation we're currently running on a possible extra-terrestrial incident in this area.'

Beth's mouth fell open. She stared at Richard MacNamarra and then turned her head to stare at Hal, who looked as stunned as she felt.

The Bureau of Paranormal Affairs? *An extra-terrestrial incident!* For one of the very few times in her life, Elizabeth Jane Cadwallader Hunter was totally (utterly, completely and absolutely) speechless.

9

'Do you have any way of proving you are who you say you are?' Hal asked the man while Beth was still floundering for some way to respond to his amazing revelation. 'Like an identity card or something?'

Richard MacNamarra smiled. 'You've been watching too many cops and robbers shows on TV,' he said. 'I have a driver's license and a few credit cards with my name on, but we don't carry cards around to show we work for the BPA, I'm just an ordinary working guy, young man. I don't carry a gun or anything like that.'

'Wh-what makes you think we might be able to help?' Beth croaked. 'With your investigation, I mean.'

Mr MacNamarra gazed out over the ocean. 'I hope you won't take offence,' he said, 'but I happened to overhear the conversation the two of you were having in the cafe back there.' His bright eyes turned to fix on Beth. 'You mentioned something about seeing a strange light out in the bay last night.'

'I sure did,' Beth breathed.

'I've seen it *twice*,' Hal said. 'Once last night, and once the night before. Beth didn't see it the first time, and she didn't believe me when I told her—'

'Hal!' Beth interrupted quickly. 'I don't think Mr MacNamarra needs to know all that stuff.'

'Call me Richard,' said the man. 'And I'll call you Beth and Hal, if that's OK?'

'Sure,' Beth said, edging closer to him along the bench. 'How can we help, Richard? Hal thinks there's some totally boring explanation for the light, but I reckon it's something *else*. Something totally out of this world.' She grinned. 'Literally!'

'That's what I've been sent here to find out,' Mr MacNamarra said. He gestured to the envelope in Hal's hand. Hal had put the pictures back in it as they had crossed the road. 'Am I right in assuming those are the pictures you took of the phenomenon, Hal? May I see them?'

Hal felt a twinge of reluctance. He wasn't one hundred per cent convinced by the man's story.

Beth scooped the envelope out of Hal's grasp and handed it over to Mr MacNamarra.

'You can't see a whole lot right now,' Beth said as Mr MacNamarra flicked quickly through the black pictures with their little green flashes. He didn't seem to notice the one with the two figures. 'We're having the best ones blown up.'

'They'll need blowing up several thousand times if you're going to make anything substantial out,' Mr MacNamarra said. 'Does your local store have the facilities to do that?'

'Mr Kowalski can do up to twelve by eight,' Hal said. 'That's the largest paper he keeps in stock.'

Richard MacNamarra shook his head. 'That's nowhere near big enough, Hal,' he said. 'We have the equipment back at base to blow this up so it would fill a billboard. And we can computer-enhance anything that shows up. With our equipment you could read the patent number on a pin head from five thousand yards.'

'Wow,' Beth breathed. 'You'd really be able to see some stuff then.'

'Look,' Mr MacNamarra said, 'what do you say I take these back to my head office right now and have my people start work on them?'

'Where's your head office?' Hal asked.

'Boston,' Mr MacNamarra said. 'My car is parked over by the Essex Building.' The Essex Building was around back of Frenchies. 'I could be back in town in two hours, and we could have all the evidence we need by the end of the day.'

'I don't know . . .' Hal said uneasily.

'I understand,' Richard MacNamarra said. 'You think I'm going to run off with your pictures and claim all the glory for myself. Well, you couldn't be more wrong. These are *your* pictures Hal, Beth, and I'm going to make darned sure everyone knows it when the story comes out. I'll tell you what, I'm going to write you out a receipt for the pictures right now.' He took out a notebook and tore a page out. Using the picture envelope as a base, he started writing.

'And I'm going to leave you my personal phone number so you can contact me any time you want.' He glanced at Beth and grinned. 'In case you see anything else.'

'You want us to keep looking?' Beth asked.

'I sure do, Beth. If not for intelligent, open-minded guys like you, the Bureau wouldn't get half the information it does.'

Beth stared at him with full-moon eyes. 'Is there real proof that aliens have landed on Earth?' she asked.

Richard MacNamarra smiled. 'I'll tell you the truth, Beth. It's like fitting together parts of a big jigsaw. Right now we can't see the whole picture, but if these,' he tapped the envelope, 'are what I think they are, then we'll be able to take a big step forward in our understanding. And it'll all be down to the two of you.'

'All the same,' Hal said, 'no offence, Mr Mac – uh, Richard, but I'm really not happy about the pictures being taken away like that.'

'Hal!' Beth snapped. 'Richard is giving us a *receipt*, for heaven's sake. He works for the government – he isn't going to rook us.'

'No, Beth,' Mr MacNamarra said, 'if Hal has a problem with this, I think we should hear him out.' The bright blue eyes turned on to Hal's face. 'OK, Hal, you tell me what your concerns are and I'll do my best to answer them. Why don't you trust me?'

Under the piercing gaze of Richard MacNamarra's eyes, Hal felt himself blush bright-red.

'I'm not saying that,' he mumbled. 'It's just that, well, they're *our* pictures. If there was anything weird going on, I wanted *us* to find out.' He looked at Beth. 'Us, on our own, without any help. *You* know what I mean, Beth.'

'Of course,' Beth said. 'And *normally* I'd totally agree with you. But this is a really, really big thing, Hal. I mean – *aliens*.' She looked at Richard MacNamarra. 'You'll get in contact with us the *second* you find anything on the pictures, promise?'

'You have my word, Beth. You have my word, Hal. I want you to give me your names and addresses, and I promise faithfully that I'll call you the moment I hear anything. And that'll probably be within five or six hours, so you'd better both make sure you're by the phone this afternoon.'

'You bet!' Beth said.

Richard MacNamarra stood up. 'And if these pictures are as important as I think they are, then the two of you will be invited down to Boston to make statements.' He grinned. 'You might even wind up on TV talk shows, telling everyone how you came up with evidence of an extra-terrestrial encounter.'

'Wow!' Beth breathed. Mr MacNamarra wrote their names and addresses and telephone numbers down in his notebook.

'You've both been a great help,' Mr MacNamarra said, shaking Hal and Beth by the hand. 'Your folks should be very proud of you.'

'I keep telling my mom that,' Beth smiled. 'But she doesn't always see it like that.'

'She will when we've finished with these,' Mr MacNamarra said as he slipped the envelope into his pocket. 'Remember, I'll be calling you this afternoon. Make sure you're at home.'

Beth watched as Richard MacNamarra loped across the road and headed around a corner toward where he'd said he'd parked his car.

'Well,' she said, 'what do you say to *that*, Hal?'

'I've never heard of the Bureau of Paranormal Affairs,' Hal said.

'Your point being?'

'How do we know it really exists?' Hal said. 'How do we know that guy was who he said he was? Beth, I think we might have just done something totally crazy.'

'Why the heck would anyone make all that stuff up?' Beth asked. 'And he *looked* genuine enough. I mean, come on, Hal, what exactly are you saying here?'

'I don't know!' Hal snapped. 'But don't you think it was kind of a coincidence that he should be sitting at the next table to us in Frenchies?'

'Not especially,' Beth said. 'It's the nicest cafe in town. Hal, you heard what he said, we could wind up famous.'

Hal shook his head. 'No,' he said, 'the more I think about it, the more sure I am that we were totally dumb to hand the negatives over.'

A sudden decision spurred Hal to action. 'It's still not too late,' he said. 'Let's catch him before he reaches his car.'

Beth was taken by surprise as Hal sprinted across the road and went chasing up the side street where Richard MacNamarra had gone.

'Hal!' With a snort of irritation, Beth ran after him. If Hal thought he was going to blow their big chance for fame and glory, by being a totally suspicious twit, then he was wrong. No way was Richard MacNamarra making all that stuff up about the Bureau of Paranormal Affairs. Why *should* he?

Hal came running full-tilt into the street that led to the impressive Colonial structure known locally as the Essex Building. He saw Richard MacNamarra climbing into a red four-door car.

'Hey!' Hal hollered, waving his arms. 'Wait up!'

Richard MacNamarra glanced up for a split second. Then he jumped into the car and slammed the door. Moments later the engine gunned and the car whiplashed out of its parking space with a scream of brakes and came hurtling toward Hal.

In the instant before the survival instinct took over, Hal realized that Richard MacNamarra had gotten into the passenger seat, and that someone else was driving.

Hal dived for the sidewalk as the car swept past, only a fraction away from his trailing legs. It was like they didn't care whether they ran over him or not.

The car sped off, tyres shrieking as it took a fast corner and careered out of sight.

Beth came running around the corner and almost fell over Hal as he sprawled breathlessly on the ground. She had heard the violent noise that the speeding car had made.

'What happened?' Beth shouted, staring in the car's wake. 'Didn't he *see* you?'

'He saw me, OK,' Hal said grimly as he picked himself up. 'He tried to make a tarmac pizza out of me!'

'Get out of here!' Beth said. 'He was probably driving fast because he wants to get back to his office as quickly as possible.'

'He wasn't driving,' Hal said.

'Huh?'

'There was already someone in the car,' Hal said. 'It was Drew! That shifty-looking guy from the quay! *He* was driving the car, Beth. I'm telling you!'

'But that doesn't make any sense,' Beth said.

Then a thought hit her like a bolt of lightning through the clouds of confusion that filled her head. She yanked the torn slip of paper out of her pocket and stared at Richard MacNamarra's phone number.

Without another word she ran to the public phone out front of the Essex Building. She fed a couple of coins into the apparatus and pressed out the number.

Hal stood next to her and Beth held the phone up so they could both hear.

The phone whirred a couple of times then clicked as someone at the other end picked up.

'Hello, Starlight Escort Agency,' said the high-pitched voice of a young woman with bad sinus trouble. 'Your pleasure is our business. This is Patti speaking. How can we be of service?'

10

In her heart, Beth already knew the answer to the question she was about to ask. But she needed to be certain. Maybe, just *maybe* Starlight Escort Agency was some kind of secret code–name for the Bureau of Paranormal Affairs.

'Could you tell me if a Mr Richard MacNamarra works there, please?' she asked.

'I think you have the wrong number, honey,' the woman squeaked in her scratchy, nasal voice. 'We don't have no men working here at all. It ain't that kind of place, honey.'

'So, you're not the Bureau of Paranormal Affairs?' Beth asked, heroically refraining from telling the woman exactly how she felt about strangers calling her *honey*.

'Is this one of those crank calls?' the woman squawked. 'Are you taping this to play back over the radio?'

'Yes,' Beth said. 'Got it in one. That's exactly what it is. You're going to be on the radio, *honey*.' She slammed the receiver down.

Hal was about to say *didn't I tell you so?*, but he changed his mind when he saw the too-angry-to-speak expression on Beth's face.

She was so mad that she felt like she could have ripped the telephone stand clear out of the sidewalk and thrown it right through the front wall of the Essex Building.

She took several long, deep, calming breaths.

'OK,' she said very slowly. 'We've just been ripped off *royally*!' She looked at Hal. 'Did you get the car license plates?'

'No,' Hal said. 'Sorry. I was kind of tied-up with getting run down.'

'No problem,' Beth said with amazing restraint. 'We have the guy's name and description, plus a description of that geek, Drew. All I have to do is call home, and my mom will have a cordon thrown around this town so tight that a *mouse* couldn't get through. Never mind a *rat* like Richard MacNamarra.'

'Are you going to tell her the whole story?' Hal asked.

'I guess I'll just have to,' Beth said as she pressed out her home number. The phone rang. It burred four times and then there was a click as the answerphone came on-line.

Beth listened to her mother's voice.

'This is Karen Hunter. I'm afraid I can't—'

Then a second voice started speaking over the answerphone message.

'Hello? Hello? Who's there? Is that you, Karen?'

'Gran!' Beth shouted into the phone. 'It's not Mom. It's me!'

An ear-shattering whine sang down the line and Beth jerked her head away from the receiver. The last thing she heard was her mom's recorded voice saying she couldn't get to the phone right now, and her gran saying, 'Darn this stupid machine, I'll just—' And then the line cut off.

She called back three or four times but the line was engaged. Whatever her gran had done to the machine, it made contact with home impossible for the time being. Besides which, Gran had asked if the caller had been Beth's mom – which made it pretty obvious to Beth that her mom wasn't at home right then.

'Now what?' Beth asked. 'Every second we waste, that low-down creeparoo is getting further and further away with our pictures.'

'Call the cops,' Hal said. 'It's the only thing to do.'

'You call them,' Beth said.

A few seconds later, Hal had gotten through to the local police station.

'I want to report a robbery,' Hal said to the person at the other end of the line. 'Huh? Oh, it's Hal. Hal Moon. Oh, hi, Officer Perch. Look, a guy just ripped me off for some pictures. Huh?'

'What's she saying?' Beth asked. Beth had met Officer Perch before.

'Shh! Yeah. Well, no, not exactly. I gave them to him, but then I thought maybe he wasn't who he said he was. Huh? Oh, right. He said he worked for the BPA. Sorry? Yeah, he said it was a government department: the Bureau of Paranormal Affairs. The guy said he was investigating an alien incident. Beth and I had taken pictures of some weird-looking lights and—' Hal stopped dead and stared at the receiver. 'Hello? Hello?'

'What happened?' Beth asked.

'She just laughed and rang off,' Hal said. 'She thought I was kidding her.'

'Ever heard the story about the boy who cried wolf?' Beth said.

'Meaning what?'

'You spend so much of your time playing jokes on people,' Beth said, 'that when you really are in trouble, no one believes you.' She squared her shoulders.

'It looks like we're on our own with this,' she said determinedly. 'At least until we can get through to my mom and I can explain the whole business to her.' She eyed Hal. 'We have some investigating to do. There are some questions I need answered. Are you coming, or are you going to just stand there fly-catching?'

Hal closed his gaping mouth. 'Where are we going?' he asked.

'Back to the quay,' Beth said. 'I want a word with that Archie guy. I want to find out *exactly* what he knows about that green light.'

Hal pursued Beth down to The Front. It was like chasing a skinny, red-headed hurricane.

'Some people sure are determined that there won't be any evidence to prove the light was out there,' he said. 'I think I can figure what happened. Drew must have gone to tell the MacNamarra guy that we were asking questions about the light and that we had pictures of it. Then Drew waited in the car while MacNamarra suckered us into handing over the pictures. And if I hadn't gotten suspicious, they'd have been home free, because the two of us would have been sitting waiting by a phone that was never gonna ring. It would have been late tonight before we even began to think there was anything screwy going on. And by then our pictures would have been long-gone.'

Beth nodded. 'This is all my fault,' she said.

'How do you figure that?'

'If I hadn't been so determined to believe it was *aliens*, we would never have handed those pictures over. The Bureau of Paranormal Affairs! Huh! I'll show that guy something *paranormal* if I see him again. I'll show him how his backside can be in New Hampshire while his *head* is in Kentucky!'

'Heck!' Hal said as they approached the quay area. 'Archie is gone.'

He was right. There was still the same level of activity down by The Whaler bar, but the grizzled old man was gone.

'Maybe he's getting another drink,' Beth said, heading toward the bar. 'I'll go check it out.'

'We can't go in there,' Hal said.

Beth looked around at him. '*Can't* isn't a word we detectives use, kid.'

'Kid? What do you mean, *kid*?' Hal said. 'I'm the same age as you.'

'Not by three days, you're not,' Beth said. 'And a lot can happen in three days.'

'What the heck does that mean?' he asked her. As she marched into the gloom of the

99

long, low bar-room, Hal was only half a pace behind her.

Corners were lit up by games machines and some sleazy-sounding music was playing low in the background. Beth didn't like the stale smell of the place, nor the eyes that peered at her as she walked up to the bar.

Hal felt like a minnow that had just swum into a sharks' nest.

'Hi,' Beth said to the man behind the bar. 'I'm looking for Archie.'

The man looked slowly around the dark room. 'He ain't here.'

'Yes, I can see that,' Beth said. 'Do you know where he went?'

'You could ask at the Mission,' the man said.

'The what?'

'The Mission. He lives at the Mission.'

'I know where he means,' Hal said.

They thanked the barman and left.

'The mission is a kind of hotel,' Hal explained as he led Beth along the street. 'A cheap kind of a hotel where people on welfare stay. It's not exactly five star, though.'

They came to a large old building that looked as if it might once have been quite grand – a century or two ago! Now, it slumped behind a screen of tall trees like a ruin waiting to fall down in a rush of rubble and a spout of dust.

Blank windows with peeling paint stared emptily at them from walls that showed years of neglect.

'I can see what you mean about it not being five star,' Beth said as she eyed the grim old hotel. 'It looks like roach heaven in there.'

The place didn't get any better once the two friends were inside. They came into a broad entrance hall painted in a grim variety of shades of *gloomy*. A man sat behind a counter, smoking a cigar and watching a small black-and-white television. From the noise, it sounded like he was watching some cacophonous gameshow.

'Excuse me,' Beth said politely. 'We're looking for a man called Archie.' She smiled her most appealing smile. 'We were told he lived here.'

'Room thirteen,' the man said without even looking away from the television.

'Could you direct us there, please?' Hal asked. At last the man looked at them. His face didn't register surprise or any kind of interest at all.

'Up the stairs,' he growled, his eyes already sliding back toward the television screen. 'Turn right. Fourth door down.'

'Thanks.'

They headed up the stairs. The fourth ill-painted brown door along on the right had the number 13 screwed to it.

'Here goes,' Beth said. She knocked.

There was a scuffling noise from inside and a suspicious voice called, 'Who's that?'

Beth brought her mouth up to the crack of the door. 'Could we speak to you?' she called. 'It's us. From the quay. You spoke to us earlier. Remember?'

Hal and Beth looked at each other in the silence that followed. Beth's eyebrows rose questioningly and Hal shrugged.

Then there was the sound of a key turning in a lock and the door edged open to reveal a slice of Archie's craggy face.

'Hi, there,' Beth said with a big smile. 'My name's Beth Hunter, and this is Hal Moon. I wonder if I could ask you a few more questions about the light we mentioned earlier.'

'I didn't see anything,' Archie slurred like a man who has had several drinks too many. 'I'm not involved, OK?'

'So you admit there's something going on?' Hal chipped in over Beth's shoulder.

'I didn't say that,' Archie mumbled.

'But you said you weren't involved,' Hal

persisted. 'What is it that you're not involved with?' Beth was nearer the open crack of the door and she was having real trouble with Archie's alcohol-breath.

'Your friend from down at the quay just tried to run Hal over,' Beth said. 'If you know anything, then I think you should tell us right now. Otherwise I'm afraid I'm going to have to go fetch my mom. And my mom is a police lieutenant. It's up to you, either you can answer a few questions now, or I go call my mom and you take a trip down to the police station as an accessory to attempted murder!'

Archie stared at her as if he couldn't believe his ears.

Then he looked at Hal.

'Is she for real?' Archie asked.

Hal nodded.

A slow grin spread over Archie's face. 'Ya got some moxie, kid, I'll give ya that. Wassya name again?'

'Beth.'

'Beth.' He nodded. 'Yeah. Well, Beth 'n' Hank—'

'Hal,' Hal said.

'Fer a start,' Archie slurred, 'Drew Bacchus ain't a nice guy to know, OK? And if ya take my advice, you'll stop asking questions about things that are nothin' to do with you.' He looked at Beth. 'Ya may come on like gang-busters, li'l lady, but you're gettin' inta some bad stuff here. Din' your daddy ever tell ya it's best ta let sleeping dogs lie?'

'No,' Beth said angrily. 'I don't believe anyone ever told me that.'

Archie looked calculatingly at her, then switched his gaze to Hal.

'Bacchus tried ta run ya down, ya say, boy?'

'That's right,' Hal said. 'Him and a guy who called himself Richard MacNamarra. The other guy had just tricked us into handing over some pictures I took of the light.'

'You've got to help us,' Beth said. 'You know what that light is, don't you? What's the big secret?'

'OK,' Archie said. 'You're already hip deep in it, so I guess ya deserve ta know the truth.' He looked at Beth. 'And maybe ya police loo-tenant momma will be able ta do somethin' about it.'

He opened the door wider and stepped back.

'Well?' he said. 'Are ya comin' in, or ain't ya? I ain't talkin' in the hallway.'

Slightly uneasily, Beth and Hal stepped over the threshold. Archie slammed the door behind them and stood with his back to it. He reached behind himself and they heard the key turn in the lock.

'I reckon we need a li'l privacy ta talk about this,' he said. When he moved away from the door, the two friends could see that the key was gone.

Beth began to have serious doubts as to whether this was one of her better ideas.

11

The room was half-dark and ruinously untidy. A blind hung across the window like a torn sail. The smell of whisky and other, more unpleasant things, hung in the stale air. Beth spotted two empty whisky bottles amongst the rubbish.

'A man's gotta make a livin',' Archie mumbled, scratching his face and shambling across to an old couch that sagged like a hammock. He slumped into it. 'But there's some things a man has ta refuse ta do.' He eyed the two friends. 'Lord only knows what ruination they're causin' out there.' He made a broad, vague gesture of his arm toward the window.

'I got seven grandchil'en,' he chuckled throatily, leaning over and wrenching a thick billfold from his back pocket. 'Wanna see some pictures?'

'No. Thanks all the same, uh, Archie,' Beth said. She wanted out of that nasty, stuffy room as quick as possible. 'Can you just tell us about the light, please.'

'I *was*,' Archie said, leaning back into the

couch. He blinked blearily at them. 'It's 'cos I got grandchil 'en that I wouldn't do it. Get me?'

'Not really,' Hal said. 'Was it some kind of *experiment*?'

'Huh?' Archie's head began to slump and his eyes became glassy.

Hal had the feeling that the guy was so tanked up on whisky that he could go unconscious on them at any moment. 'Was it an experiment?' Hal asked again. 'Did something go wrong?'

'Nope,' Archie mumbled, his chin on his chest. 'Weren't no 'speriment. Them Webcore people don't care nothin' for nobody.'

'I'm sorry?' Beth said, edging closer to the man, who seemed to be collapsing in on himself like a slowly deflating balloon. 'What did you say?'

'I wouldn't do it,' Archie mumbled, his voice getting gradually less and less coherent.

'What wouldn't you do?' Hal asked.

Archie's eyes swam closed and his breathing deepened.

Beth stood with her fists on her hips. 'He's as drunk as a skunk!' she said.

'He must have been hitting the bottle like crazy after we first spoke to him,' Hal said. 'And what was that about *Webcore*?'

'Beats me. What's a webcore?'

'It's that factory up-river from here,' Hal said. 'Haven't you seen the news? There's some kind of problem up there with some environmental group.'

Beth snapped her fingers. 'That's right,' she said. 'Mom was talking about it the other day. What were they called? Seventh Heaven? No, that's not right.'

'They're called Seventh Wave,' Hal said. 'Hold on! I think he's saying something.' Archie was mumbling to himself. Hal decided this was no time to be squeamish. The semi-conscious man clearly knew *something*. If the two of them were going to find out *what* then they'd need to be quick, before he passed out completely.

Hal stepped over an empty whisky bottle and leaned close to the man. With a grimace of distaste he shook Archie's shoulder.

'Don't go down ta The Grifts,' Archie shouted, making both of them jump at the sudden noise. 'Not safe. I got grandchil 'en ta think of.' His voice faded again to a cavernous rumble, so that Hal had to lean really close to catch what he was saying. 'Fouling up the world, they are. They don't care. I don't want nothin' ta do with it. Leave me outta it. I ain't gonna say nothin' ta nobody. Jus' lee' me outta it . . .'

That was it. Archie began to snore steadily. Hal straightened up and looked at Beth.

'Do you have the *slightest* idea what all that was about?' Beth asked him.

'The Grifts is what some people call those old abandoned factory sheds down by the river,' Hal said.

Beth knew the place he meant. The Monasaukee River ran along the north flank of town. Near its mouth, an algae-green old wooden footbridge spanned its slow, brown width. On the far bank, derelict industrial buildings were being engulfed by the forest. People were warned to steer clear of the place – apparently it was rotting away and a roof or a wall was liable to come tumbling down on a person's head if they ventured inside any of the worksheds.

'So,' Beth said, 'there's something going on at The Grifts, and somehow, that Webcore factory is involved.' She looked at Hal in the gloom. 'Is that what he was saying?'

'I guess so,' Hal said. 'Let's get out of here. We need to think all this over.'

Beth moved over to the door and twisted the handle.

'Rats,' she said, remembering. 'He locked it. Did you see where he put the key?'

'Nope,' Hal said, looking down at the snoring old man. 'In his pocket, I guess. Uh, wanna check it out?'

'No way!'

'Well, one of us has to,' Hal said. 'Unless you want to stay here until he wakes up again.'

'I am *not* putting my hand in his pocket,' Beth said uncompromisingly. 'You do it.'

'Why me?'

'Because I'm a girl and you're a boy.'

Hal stared at her. 'Do you want to run that past me again?' he said. 'Since when has being a *girl* made any difference to how you act?'

'Oh, *fine*, Hal! Why don't we just stand here arguing about it for a while, huh? I mean it's not like we're in any kind of a *hurry* or anything. It's not like some guy just stole our pictures and tried to run you over or anything. I mean—'

'OK! OK!' Hal shouted. 'Quit it, will you? I'll look for the key.' He reached out a tentative hand toward the slumbering man. 'Yuck!' he muttered under his breath. 'And I'm still going to want to know why a *girl* can't do this.'

Loud footsteps echoed in the corridor. Hal and Beth looked at one another and then at the door.

A heavy fist beat on the door.

'Hey! Archie! Open up, we want to talk to you.'

110

Beth and Hal stood frozen in silence. Neither of them needed to say anything; they both recognised the gravelly voice.

'Archie! It's Drew! Open up! I'm not going to hurt you. We just need to talk. *Archie!*' The door shook under a renewed assault.

'Are you sure they're in there?' asked a second voice. Beth's hair almost stood on end. It was the suave, sophisticated *lying* voice of the man who called himself Richard MacNamarra. 'Might he and the kids have gotten out a back way?'

'The only way out is past Pug Henry down in the hall,' Drew said. 'And he said the two kids came up but didn't come back down. They're in there all right. You want I should break the door down?'

Hal and Beth stared at each other in near-panic. The two men knew they were in there, and they were prepared to smash their way in to get at them. This was not a good situation to be in! Not at all.

'No, wait!' Richard MacNamarra said. 'Beth? Hal?' he called. 'Can you hear me? I know you're in there with Archie. Listen, guys, I don't know what the old man's been telling you, but you shouldn't believe him. Archie gets confused, OK? Now what say you open the door so we can have a pow-wow? There are some things I need to explain.'

'Yeah!' Beth yelled. 'Like why you lied to us and stole our property! *And* why you tried to run Hal down, you total creep!'

Hal gave a groan of despair. So much for his hope that the two men could be tricked into thinking they'd already left the building.

'Ah, Beth. Hello again. Listen, Beth, I had to be economical with the truth back there,' Richard MacNamarra said smoothly. 'It was for your own good. There were some things that I thought you'd be safer not knowing.' There was a brief pause during which Hal and Beth exchanged uneasy glances.

'I guess I underestimated you,' Mr MacNamarra continued. 'I guess you're both just too smart to be kept in the dark, huh?'

'You can say that again!' Beth shouted.

Someone pounded again on the door and Drew shouted: 'Archie! Open this door or I'll break every bone in your body!'

'Shut it!' Richard MacNamarra hissed. 'Keep that fat mouth of yours *shut*.'

'Archie can't come to the door right now,' Hal called. 'He's taking a little nap. And if you think we're going to open the door while that crazy man is out there, you can think again!' A sudden thought struck Hal. He ran over to the window and yanked the torn blind aside. Dust showered down. Hal found himself looking out over empty grounds hemmed by trees. There was no one to shout to – no one to call for help. He tried hauling up the windowsash, but it wouldn't budge.

'Drew?' they heard Richard MacNamarra say, 'I want you to go wait in the car.' There was the sound of footsteps retreating along the hall.

'Drew has gone,' Richard MacNamarra called through the door. 'Will you talk to me now?'

Beth looked around for some way out. She pointed toward a side door and Hal went to check it out.

'I'll talk,' Beth called. 'What do you want to talk about, *Richard*? If that's really your name. Do you want to talk about Webcore? Or maybe you'd like to talk about what's happening over at The Grifts?'

'Ah.' The voice was as controlled as ever through the wooden panels of the door. 'I see Archie has been telling you things. You see, the truth is, Beth, Archie doesn't know what's really going on out there. Archie drinks, Beth, as I guess you've found out. We couldn't trust him. We had to feed him some disinformation, Beth. Do you know what *disinformation* is?'

'Sure,' Beth called, 'it's a smart-aleck word for *lying*.'

Hal came out of Archie's tiny, grimy bedroom. He shook his head. The window was nailed shut in there. Hal spread his arms helplesly. Beth lifted her fist to her ear, finger and thumb outstretched in the *telephone* gesture.

Hal nodded and began to search. Archie didn't seem like the kind of guy who would have a telephone, but it was worth taking a look.

'I figure it's time I laid all my cards out on the table,' Richard MacNamarra said. 'The truth is, Beth, we didn't need your pictures.'

'So why steal them?' Beth shouted. She stepped over the debris to where Archie lay crumpled on the couch. Maybe if she could rouse the drunken man, he'd be able to help them out. Maybe! She grabbed two handfulls of his sweater and shook him as hard as she could. He spluttered and snorted, but his eyes remained firmly shut, although his mouth was dribbling open.

'I was ordered to retrieve them,' Richard MacNamarra said. 'The people I work for didn't want any loose cannons, Beth. We had to make sure there was no physical evidence of the crash.'

Beth stopped dead.

'What crash?' she called. Hal was also poised in alert silence.

'We tracked the UFO all the way from New Brunswick,' Richard MacNamarra said. 'We had it on radar all the way along the coast. Then it vanished clear off the screen over New Greenwich.'

'You're lying!' Hal shouted.

'I'm not lying to you, Hal, I promise,' Richard MacNamarra said. 'What you saw last night was a retrieval squad picking up the pieces of a downed UFO. We took the wreckage over to The Grifts.'

Beth's hands came up over her mouth.

'That is just such a load of baloney!' Hal shouted.

'No, wait,' Beth said. 'Hey?' she called in a trembling voice. 'Did you find any . . . uh, I mean . . . did you find the pilot of the UFO?'

'I can't tell you that,' Richard MacNamarra said. 'That's classified, Beth. In fact, the whole clear-up operation is classed A1 confidential, Beth. I'm really sticking my neck out by telling you this at all. But I figure you deserve to know the truth, guys.'

'Prove that you're telling the truth!' Hal shouted. 'There are no such things as UFOs – not from other planets, anyhow. There would be real proof by now, if we were being visited by people from outer space.'

'Wake up and smell the coffee, Hal!' Richard MacNamarra called. 'Welcome to the real world! There *is* proof, we just don't go around *shouting* about it. Now, look. This is crazy. Open the door, guys. I promise I won't hurt you.'

'You nearly ran me over!' Hal yelled.

'That was a stupid mistake, Hal,' Richard MacNamarra said. 'Sometimes we need to employ stupid people. I never wanted that to happen. Now, look, let's be sensible about this. One way or another you guys have got to come out of there. All I want to do is to have you meet some of the people I work for. Government people, Beth, Hal. What do you say?'

'We're not going anywhere with you,' Beth called.

'Agreed,' Richard MacNamarra said. 'But what I want you to do is to come on out of there. Then we'll call your folks and have them meet us here. It's really important that you understand the need for total security until we can take the UFO wreckage somewhere safe. Can you imagine what would happen if word got out that there was a crashed UFO over in The Grifts? The press would be all over us like a rash. And then there'd be rubberneckers from every town in two hundred miles! Evidence would be destroyed in the rush.'

Beth gnawed her lower lip. Could he be telling the truth? She thought of the two blurry figures in Hal's picture, and of the strange person she had battled on the beach. Could they be the pilot and crew of a real UFO? She looked at the door and then into Hal's determinedly sceptical face. Then she looked down at Archie. She saw the tail of a key protruding from his pants pocket. She reached over and tugged it out.

Hal moved toward her. 'Beth, no!' he said.

Beth stretched a cautionary hand out to him as she walked slowly to the door.

'Listen, Richard, or whatever your name is,' Beth said, her head close to the door. 'I don't know whether you're telling me the truth or not, but I guess I'm going to have to trust you.'

'Good girl, Beth,' Richard MacNamarra crooned through the door. 'Now open the door. That's the sensible thing to do.'

'I don't know about *sensible*,' Beth said as she inserted the key in the lock. 'But I do need to talk to someone about what I saw last night. Because, whatever *you're* up to, I think I saw an alien out there, and I really need to talk it through with someone.'

'Beth,' Hal said, coming up behind her. 'I really don't think this is a good idea.'

'Do you know of some other way out?' Beth asked him.

Hal swallowed a lump in his throat. 'I guess not.'

'Right!'

Beth turned the key and drew the door open. Richard MacNamarra's foot came swinging into the gap, sending the door flying wide and taking the two of them by surprise.

'Like I said,' Richard MacNamarra growled, a dangerous light in his eyes. 'Welcome to the real world.'

There was a gun in his hand, levelled straight at Beth's forehead.

12

The man who called himself Richard MacNamarra smiled a sinister smile from behind the brutal black shape of his gun.

'You liar!' Beth shouted. 'There never was any crashed UFO!'

'Nope,' Richard MacNamarra said with a twitch of his lip. 'There never was, Beth. But you only have yourself to blame. If I hadn't overheard you talking about aliens back in the cafe, I'd never have come up with the idea of the Bureau of Paranormal Affairs.'

'Smart work, Beth,' Hal muttered. 'Real smart.'

'Now, here's what we're going to do,' Richard MacNamarra said as calmly as ever. 'We're going to walk out of here, real cool and easy.' His eyes flashed danger. 'And we're not going to make any fuss or give anyone the idea that there's anything wrong. Do I make myself clear?'

'You won't get away with this,' Beth said.

Richard MacNamarra frowned and shook his head. 'I'm disappointed, Beth,' he said with an ironic smile. 'I'd have expected something a little more original from you.'

'Well, try this,' Beth said. 'You're a dirty rotten, low-down, lying toad-rat-skunk-weasel *creep*, and my mom is gonna put you behind bars for the rest of your life if you don't wise up and let us go right now.'

Richard MacNamarra's smile froze.

'That mouth of yours is going to get you into a whole heap of trouble, Beth,' he said. 'I recommend you keep it shut.' He gestured with the gun. 'Now. Both of you. Walk!'

Hal gave Beth a look which he hoped she would realize meant: *keep quiet and do what he says*. When Beth's temper was up she didn't always think too carefully about the consequences of her actions. It was something that Hal had always admired about her, but right then he was afraid it might get them both shot.

But Beth wasn't crazy enough to disobey a man who had a gun held up to her head. She was scared. She was more scared than she'd ever been in her life. But one thing was preventing her from coming apart at the seams: she was determined to show a brave face to the gunman. However bad she felt inside, she wasn't going to let him see it on her face. No way!

Richard MacNamarra steered the two friends along the corridor and down the stairs. The gameshow was still cranking out its endless din down in the reception hallway.

Richard MacNamarra slid his gun into the pocket of his jacket as they came out into clear, clean daylight. The car was parked nearby. Drew was leaning against the fender, smoking a cigarette.

'Put that filthy thing out and get in the car,' Richard MacNamarra snapped. Drew obeyed with a sullen look. Beth and Hal were crammed into the back. Drew got into the driver's seat and Richard MacNamarra climbed in next to him.

He leaned over the back of the seat.

'One stupid move from either of you . . .' He made a small, sharp gesture with the gun. His meaning was perfectly clear.

'Where are you taking us?' Hal asked.

'You'll find out.' Richard MacNamarra flicked his fingers toward the half-grown-over exit to the road and Drew started the car.

'Do you have any idea how bad smoking is for you?' Richard MacNamarra asked Drew. 'Do you know how many people die every year from smoking-related disease?'

In the mirror, Beth saw Drew give Richard

MacNamarra an uneasy glance.

'Hey, cool it, man,' Drew said. 'Don't start getting mad at me – I've done everything you've told me to do.'

They came out into the street.

'I told you to dump the stuff,' Richard MacNamarra said. 'I didn't tell you to put on a freaking firework display out there.'

Beth's mystery antennae pricked up. She glanced at Hal. He gave a brief nod to show he had figured what they were talking about.

'Look, I ain't no scientist,' Drew said. 'A guy tells me to dump some stuff, I dump it. No-one said nothing to me about the stuff catching fire in the air. Catching fire out of *nothing*.'

Hal realized they must be talking about some chemical like phosphorus. *That* stuff burst into flames if it was exposed to oxygen. He knew about it, because sometimes his dad used it for special effects work. And Hal knew that it was dangerous stuff. Deadly dangerous.

'You were told to get rid of it out in the bay,' Richard MacNamarra growled. 'I expected you to use your intelligence and take your boat out into open water. No one said anything to you about pouring the stuff out. You were supposed to just throw the barrels overboard.'

'OK, OK,' Drew said. 'The next shipment goes way out in the bay and stays in the barrels. No problem. No one's gonna see nothin'. Everything's cool.'

'No problem?' Richard MacNamarra said. 'No *problem*? It may have escaped your notice, but we already have two big problems.' Richard MacNamarra glanced over his shoulder. 'And they're sitting right behind you.'

Beth and Hal didn't need to think too hard to figure out what he meant. Things were finally beginning to make sense. Drew was working for Richard MacNamarra. He'd been hired to take some barrels of inflammable chemicals out to sea and get rid of them in secret. But he'd cut corners. He'd only taken his boat out a short distance, well on the landward side of Cranberry Island.

That had been mistake number one.

Mistake number two had been to open the barrels. Although she didn't have Hal's background knowledge, Beth had already guessed that some sort of chemical reaction had taken place out there. A reaction which had caused the weird green light.

'OK, you two,' Richard MacNamarra growled. 'Get right down, low as you can. I don't want anyone seeing you.'

Beth and Hal folded themselves up in the cramped space in front of their seat. Hal felt a harsh hand press down on his head.

'Keep down, boy,' Richard MacNamarra snarled.

Hal let out a breathless grunt of acquiescence as he jack-knifed himself up next to Beth on the floor of the car. Her hand reached out and briefly squeezed his.

The car swung north and headed across town. It was agonising for Hal and Beth to think of all those familiar sights and all those familiar, friendly people out there, oblivious to the fact that they were huddled in the car and in terrible danger.

They were kept crushed breathlessly down there for maybe fifteen minutes.

'OK, you can come up now,' Richard MacNamarra said at last.

Beth and Hal unfolded themselves and stretched back on to the seat. The car was passing through woodland. Hal glanced over his shoulder. More trees, hemming the road in. The view through the windscreen at the front was the same.

Then the scene opened up and they drove across the main Monasaukee River Bridge. Now Hal knew exactly where he was. They were heading north on the road that snaked up through Grifts

Wood and joined on to the through-route to Portsmouth.

Drew spun the wheel to the right. For a second, Beth thought he was driving them smack into the trees, but then she saw the narrow dirt track snaking ahead of them under the brown and gold canopy of leaves.

She drew a map in her head. They were in the woods, driving, she guessed, parallel to the river and heading east, toward the coast.

After a while the trees thinned a little and the track broadened out. Hal and Beth could see signs of previous occupation: rusted machinery and fallen timber and heaps and scatterings of broken industrial equipment.

They were entering The Grifts. The roofs of the old sheds and shacks and workshops lifted over the creeping undergrowth like pieces of shipwreck at low tide.

Drew brought the car to a standstill.

Richard MacNamarra got out and opened the back door. Beth climbed out. It had gotten very dark. Under the shield of leaves through the wood, they hadn't seen the stormclouds building up across the sky. Now they could see the big dark thunderheads riding the north wind, and feel the occasional lash of a heavy, windswept raindrop.

'Looks like a storm,' Drew said. 'I'm not dumping any of that stuff out there tonight if there's a storm coming up. It'll be too dangerous."

But Richard MacNamarra wasn't paying any attention to Drew. He was staring at another car, parked behind a nearby shed so that only its rear quarter showed. A long, luxurious black limousine with tinted windows and chrome that shone in the failing light.

Beth saw a look that was either annoyance or unease pass quickly over Richard MacNamarra's face.

A man in a chauffeur's uniform and peaked cap stepped into view and opened the back door of the limousine. A man got out. An elderly man with long, swept back silver hair. He was wearing a heavy black overcoat and walked with an ebony stick as he made his way slowly across the rutted ground with the tall chauffeur at his side.

Hal and Beth looked at one another. Who the heck was *this* old man? Some rich guy, obviously, but what was he doing here?

Richard MacNamarra stepped forwards.

'Mr Downey,' he said in a nervous voice. 'This isn't what we'd agreed . . .'

The old man stopped about a yard away from Richard MacNamarra and stared first at him, then at Drew, who was still in the driver's seat, and finally at the two friends. Up close his scraggy face reminded Beth of pictures she'd seen of Aztec demon-masks: the skin drawn in under jutting cheekbones and the eyes deep-set in darkness.

'I came to see how you were progressing with your work,' the old man wheezed in a voice as thin and as cracked as black ice. He lifted his stick and jabbed it toward Hal and Beth. 'Who are these children?'

'They found out about the work we were doing,' Richard MacNamarra said. 'They were snooping around. They took some pictures.' He put his hand into his inside jacket pocket and took out Hal's envelope.

The old man made a small gesture and the chauffeur stepped forward and took the envelope. The old man went through the pictures.

'How did you let this happen?' Mr Downey asked, fixing Richard MacNamarra with a glinting eye. 'I trusted you to do a good, clean job for me.' He thrust the pictures into his coat pocket. 'You messed up, Mr MacNamarra.'

'It wasn't my fault,' Richard MacNamarra said.

'I've been working with a moron out here. He didn't follow my instructions. He—' A fierce look from the old man silenced him.

'It seems my faith in you was misplaced, Mr MacNamarra,' Mr Downey wheezed.

'Not at all, Mr Downey,' Richard MacNamarra said. 'I can fix things. Leave it to me. The rest of the stuff will go tonight.'

'And what about the children?' Mr Downey asked. 'Because you were stupid enough to bring them here, they now know of *my* involvement in this matter.' Those pictures are nothing. No one would have made any connection with Webcore because of *those*. But now they have enough knowledge to cause problems. They'll need to be dealt with, Mr MacNamarra.' The freezing old eyes swept again over Hal and Beth. 'They'll need to be dealt with *permanently*.'

'Leave it to me, Mr Downey,' Richard MacNamarra said.

With a snort, the old man turned and walked slowly back to the car, the silent chauffeur at his side as if ready to catch the frail old man if he stumbled.

At the open car door he turned. His breathless, wheezing voice came faintly back to them over the growing howl of the wind.

'Kill them, Mr MacNamarra,' he called. 'Kill them both.'

Hal and Beth drew close together, clasping hands in fear as Richard MacNamarra turned toward them and slid his hand inside his jacket to grip the handle of the gun that he had thrust into his belt.

13

With hardly a sound, the long black limousine moved out of sight behind the shack. A few moments later it glided along the dirt track down which Beth and Hal had just been brought. The tinted windows gave no hint of the terrible old man who lurked inside like some wicked old spider.

The car slid into the trees and was gone.

Richard MacNamarra seemed to relax. His hand fell away from the gun that was tucked into his belt. Despite the cold wind, Beth could see sweat trickling down his face. Whoever that old guy was, he sure gave Richard MacNamarra the shakes.

The only sound was the oppressive rustle of the wind through dry leaves. It sounded ominous to Beth: like the stealthy sounds of predators moving in for the kill.

The two friends looked round as Drew got out of the car that had brought them here. He stared at the three of them over the roof.

'You ain't really gonna kill them, are you?' he asked Richard MacNamarra. 'They're just kids.'

Richard MacNamarra looked at Hal and Beth.

'Not right now,' he said. 'We've got work to do.'

Beth shuddered. The two men were going to get rid of the chemicals first. But then what?

'Who was that guy?' Drew asked in an awed voice.

'I know who he is,' Hal said. 'He's the Chairman of the Board of Webcore. I've seen his picture in the papers. His name's Horace Downey.'

'Got it in one, kid,' Richard MacNamarra said.

Beth looked calculatingly at Richard MacNamarra. 'I'm surprised a man like you would take orders from a wrinkled old fossil like that.'

Richard MacNamarra smiled. 'You'd be amazed who I'd take orders from if they paid me as much as that wrinkled old fossil is paying me,' he said.

'What is it exactly that he's asked you to get rid of?' Hal asked.

'No more questions,' Richard MacNamarra said. He turned to Drew.

'Take them over to the wharf, there's some rope in there. Tie them up.' He gave Drew a contemptuous look. 'I take it you know how to tie a tight knot?'

Drew nodded wordlessly.

Richard MacNamarra dismissed him with a curt flick of the wrist. Drew circled the car and pushed Hal and Beth toward the sheds. Beth heard Richard speak. She glanced around. He was talking into a mobile phone.

'I'm finished here,' she heard him say. 'One more load and the job's done. Yeah, then I'll collect the rest of the money and . . .' But that was all she heard before Drew shoved her around the corner of one of the sheds and Richard MacNamarra's voice dropped out of earshot.

Hal looked around at Drew.

'Do you know what's really going on here?' he asked.

'Don't ask no questions,' Drew said, 'don't get told no lies.'

'But don't you want to know what it is that they're getting you to dump out in the bay?' Hal asked. 'I mean, if I made my living from taking people out fishing, I'd sure want to know what kind of junk was being dumped in the sea. What if it killed all the fish?'

'I'm not too curious when a man pays me a whole season's money for one week's work,' Drew said. 'Anyhow, you'll see what the stuff is soon enough, boy.'

They came to one of the larger sheds that stood right at the riverside. The wharf was crawling with green algae and the boards looked rotten enough to crumble away at a touch. Under the massing cloud, the Monasaukee river looked as grey as slate.

Beth gazed out at the narrow wooden bridge that spanned the river-mouth. On the far side, beyond that obscuring barrier of trees, was New Greenwich. Her own home was only a little distance along the coast. But the way things were shaping up, it might as well have been on the moon.

A motorboat was moored at the wharf, bobbing in the choppy, wind-tormented water like a restless horse on a bridle.

For a fleeting second, Beth was certain she saw two slender, grey shapes flit amongst the trees on the far side of the river. She looked harder, but the silvery figures were gone almost before she could focus on them.

Drew hauled open a wide, creaking door and pushed the two friends into the shed. Beth could see that it had been a warehouse. It was one big room, mostly empty now, except for a collection of about a dozen large black oildrums which stood against the wall over to their left.

'Get over there,' Drew ordered, shoving Beth and Hal toward the barrels. A smell wafted on the air. A smell so bizarre in the circumstances, that Beth thought maybe her senses were deceiving her. It was the smell of new-mown hay. And it grew stronger the closer they got to the metal barrels.

As they circled the barrels, Beth let out a gasp. Two people in thick protective cover-alls lay dead on the floor. But the growing gloom of the unlit old shed had fooled her. When she looked closer, she saw that the suits were empty. There were no faces inside the clear plastic visors on the front of the helmets.

Drew picked up a length of rope and snicked it in two with a pocket-knife.

'You don't have to do this,' Beth said to him as he came up and pulled her arms together behind her. 'Listen. People are going to start looking for us real soon. Why don't you let us go? We'll tell the police you helped us. That way, you won't spend the next ten years in jail for kidnapping. Ouch!' The rope dug into her wrists.

'I ain't listening,' Drew said as he worked on the knots, keeping one eye always on Hal.

'What do you think is going to happen next? When you've finished the job?' Beth asked.

'Richard is going to take the money and run. But what are *you* going to do?'

'I'm going on a vacation,' Drew said. 'I'm going to buy myself a car and I'm going to drive that sucker clear across the country until I hit Las Vegas. Then I'm going to have a good time, that's what I'm going to do, kid. And I ain't never coming back.'

'Wrong,' Beth said. 'I'll tell you what's going to happen. Has Richard paid you yet?' Beth twisted her head to try and look at Drew. 'I bet he hasn't paid you yet.'

Suddenly, Drew spun her around so she was facing him.

'What are you getting at, girl?'

'So, he *hasn't* paid you,' Hal said. He could see that Beth was working on Drew. He wasn't altogether sure what Beth had in mind, but he was ready to back her up.

'I bet he's told you that he'll pay you when the job is finished,' Beth said. 'And you believed him. Huh! Like, *I'd* really trust a guy like that.'

Drew stared at her.

'Don't you get it?' Beth said. 'You're going to be left swinging in the wind. Why would he bother paying you off when he can take all the money and run?'

Drew's dark eyes narrowed. 'I'd find him.'

'Oh, sure,' Beth said. 'No way! He's going to leave you to take the rap. Trust me, my mom's a police lieutenant, I *know* these things.'

'It's true,' Hal said, slowly edging around behind Drew, with escape on his mind. 'You'd better listen to her. She knows what she's talking about.'

'Face it,' Beth said, 'you're going to be in one whole heap of trouble if you don't listen to what I have to say.'

Drew glowered at her, but she could tell that the seeds she was planting were taking root in his slow mind. Now all she had to do was tie up the package and put a big red bow on top.

'Here's the thing,' she said, licking her dry lips as she went for the kill. 'People know we went to speak to Archie. How long is he going to keep his mouth shut, do you think? And then they'll know that *you're* involved. Do you want to spend the rest of your life in jail?'

'You'll have nothing,' Hal added. 'You'll wind up behind bars, and Richard—'

'Richard will what?' Richard MacNamarra stood in the doorway. 'What's going on here? Why aren't they both tied up by now?'

'When do I get my money?' Drew snarled, glaring at Richard MacNamarra.

'At the time we agreed,' Richard MacNamarra said. 'When the job is done.'

'I want my money *now*,' Drew shouted.

Richard MacNamarra walked slowly toward him. 'What's the trouble here, Drew?' he said smoothly. 'Don't you trust me?'

Drew turned to confront Richard MacNamarra, but he was too slow. Richard MacNamarra pounced, fast as a wildcat. Beth stumbled backwards as Drew fell.

'Do we have a problem here?' Richard MacNamarra snarled. 'Do we have a discontented workforce situation here?'

'I just want my money,' Drew gasped.

'And you'll get it,' Richard MacNamarra snapped. 'When *I* get it. When the job is through.' He hauled the dishevelled and subdued man to his feet.

Hal spotted something that glinted metallically in the dirt where Drew had fallen. Something that might come in useful.

'Now,' Richard MacNamarra growled. 'Get these kids tied up, and let's get this stuff shifted before the storm arrives.'

There were no further chances for Beth to work

on Drew. She didn't dare speak in front of Richard MacNamarra. Hal and Beth were tied by the wrists and ankles and dumped on the ground beside the two protective suits.

'They're going to find us,' Beth yelled angrily. 'And they're going to put you in *prison*!'

'Gag her,' Richard MacNamarra said. 'Gag them both.'

Drew tied a length of cloth around each of their mouths while Richard MacNamarra picked up one of the protective suits and started to climb into it.

'This time, I'm coming with you,' he said to Drew. 'To make sure you do the job the way I told you.'

'It's too early,' Drew said. 'We can't go out in daylight. Someone will see us.'

'I don't think so,' Richard MacNamarra said. 'Everyone will be too busy getting home before the storm hits. We'll go out beyond the island. Two trips should do it. And then we're out of here. Get kitted out and let's get moving.'

Hal and Beth watched as the two men climbed into the protective suits. In other circumstances it might almost have been funny, the way they lumbered about in the big enveloping suits like a couple of dopey bears.

They tipped the barrels one by one and rolled them out through the door.

The two men took half of the barrels. They were obviously stowing them on board the motorboat.

At last, Richard MacNamarra came in alone and stood looking down at them through the perspex visor of his helmet. From outside, they clearly heard a motor start up, and the familiar churn of agitated water.

'We'll be back,' Richard MacNamarra said, his voice muffled by the suit. 'Now don't you two kids get up to any mischief while we're gone, hear?'

Beth struggled a little and gave him a deadly glare. He laughed and walked out, pulling the door closed behind him.

Beth listened as the sound of the motor increased and then, slowly, began to fade. The two men had cast off and were heading out into the bay with their secret cargo of chemicals.

Beth heard a scuffling and a scraping sound. She twisted her head. Hal was writhing around like the severed end of an eel.

She made a guttural noise in her throat. What the heck was he doing? He was rolling in the dirt. What on earth for? Did he plan on rolling all the way into town, or what? What they needed to do was come up with some way of untying Drew's knots. So long as they were bound, they were helpless.

Hal ignored Beth's head-gestures and attempts at gagged speech. He knew exactly where he was heading. Toward the thing that had fallen out of Drew's pocket when Richard MacNamarra had jumped him.

Hal squirmed and wriggled across the floor, digging in with his heels and searching the ground with his hands.

Beth stared at him in complete confusion. Had he gone crazy? Hal had turned on to his back and he was shoving himself along the ground with his feet.

Got it! Hal would have yelled in triumph if he hadn't been gagged. He felt the small pocket-knife under his fingers. He turned half on to his side and blindly worked on getting the blade open. Twice he dropped the knife and had to find it all over again, but the third time was the charm!

The blade clicked open and Hal began the slow, difficult business of sawing through his bonds.

The way he was lying meant that Beth still couldn't see what he was doing. She made some more strangulated noises and head-shakes. She was trying to communicate to him that he should crawl over to her so they could get back to back and try to undo each other's knots. The way Beth saw it, that was their only hope of escape.

It was getting darker by the minute. Out in the open, the thunderclouds were gathering and massing like a great herd of ghostly buffalo above the trees. Rain began to bounce off the roof like iron pellets.

Hal gave a grunt as one last tug snapped the final few strands of the rope that held his wrists. He sat up and dragged the gag down.

'It's OK!' he yelled to Beth. 'I'm free!'

He hacked through the rope that held his ankles and then scrambled across to where Beth lay.

He loosened her gag and got to work at her wrists.

'Hal, you're a genius!' Beth gasped. 'Where did the knife come from?' Hal snicked his way through her ankle-ropes.

'Drew dropped it,' Hal laughed. 'Great, huh?'

But his joy was interrupted by the creak of the warehouse door being thrust open. Both of them jerked their heads around.

The door was ajar.

There was a flash of lightning and an almost immediate blast of thunder from right overhead.

Silhouetted in the doorway was a small, slender figure in grey.

Beth's heart jumped into her mouth.

She recognised the shape. And this time there could be no mistake. No possible mistake.

There were the huge black eyes and the small, eerily pale triangular face. Without a shadow of a doubt, Hal and Beth were in the presence of the person they had encountered the other night down on the beach.

They were staring into the face of someone not of this world.

14

Beth stared at the alien shape like a rabbit mesmerised by headlights on a road. She felt totally blown away, as if a crack had opened up in the world she knew and a whole universe of incredible possibilities had been revealed.

Hal knelt at her side, still as stone. Beth wasn't sure if the loud throbbing in her ears was the hammering of his heart or of her own.

Suddenly a beam of white light burst from the alien's hand. It shone around the warehouse, dust dancing in the strong beam as the pool of light traced across the floor.

They have flashlights in outer space, Beth thought dazedly. *Far out!*

The light flashed in Beth and Hal's faces. They lifted their arms to protect their eyes. There was a gasp of surprise from the figure at the door as the flashlight beam was trained steadily on the two blinded friends.

'We won't hurt you,' Beth shouted into the glare of the light. 'We're friendly.'

'What the hell are you two kids doing in here?'

'Wha-a-at?' Beth shrieked. The *alien* had spoken in perfect English. The voice was of a young woman, speaking with a strong Boston accent.

'It's dangerous in here, you idiots,' the alien said.

'Will you get that *light* out of my eyes!' Beth shouted.

The beam was switched sideways and the grey figure came toward the two friends, moving with the smooth grace of an athlete.

Up closer, they could see that the grey clothing was a hooded sweatshirt and a pair of leggings. The *alien* raised a hand to her head and pulled her face off.

Beth was only a split second away from passing out with shock when she saw a perfectly ordinary human face staring out at them from inside the raised hood. The woman brushed the hood back to reveal close-cropped dark hair.

'Who *are* you?' Beth breathed.

But the woman's attention was focussed on the few remaining barrels that still stood against the wall. She ran the flashlight beam over them.

'Got them!' she said. 'We've finally got them!'

'Hey!' Beth yelled. 'What's the big idea of

parading around pretending to be some kind of creature from outer space?'

'Sorry?' The woman seemed totally distracted by the barrels of chemicals.

Beth jumped up to confront the woman.

'You attacked me on the beach last night!' she said. Yes, it was definitely *her*. The woman was only slightly above Beth's height – a good size for a twelve year old, but very short for a woman who seemed to be in her late teens or early twenties.

The woman stared at Beth and a sudden realization dawned in her eyes.

'You again!' she said. 'What are you talking about? *You* attacked *me*.'

'I thought you were *him*,' Beth said, waving a hand at Hal. 'You tried to strangle me!'

'I thought you were from Webcore,' the young woman said. 'We knew they were up to something. I'd just caught sight of the fire out on the water when you jumped on me. You're lucky I didn't break your neck.'

'So, what's with the alien routine?' Beth asked.

'The mask was in case I was seen,' the young woman explained. 'I didn't want to be recognized. I wasn't pretending to be an *alien*. It was just something I bought at a novelty store.'

'Where's the other one?' Beth asked. 'Your friend.'

The woman stared at her. 'What friend? I'm working solo.'

'Excuse me for butting in!' Hal shouted, 'but shouldn't we be having this conversation somewhere else? There's a guy out there with a loaded gun and a really unfriendly attitude.'

'He's right,' the woman said. 'We need to get clear of these chemicals. Can you smell it? The smell like cut hay? That's phosgene.'

'What the heck is *phosgene*?' Beth demanded. 'And who are you, and what's going on around here?'

The woman frowned at her. 'What is going on around here, is that Webcore are trying to dump this stuff before the FBI move in on them,' she said, brandishing the flashlight at the barrels. 'And as for who I am: I'm a member of Seventh Wave. We've been monitoring Webcore for the past eight months. And *phosgene* is an incredibly dangerous chemical! Now, are we going to get out of here, or what?'

'In what way, dangerous?' Hal gasped.

'Breathe it and you're dead,' the woman said. 'Trust me!'

'Hal! Quit asking questions and move it!' Beth yelled. 'You heard the lady!'

The young woman led them out into a teeming rainstorm.

'This way,' she said, running swiftly over to the right. They followed her in under the rusted corrugated iron roof of a one-walled shelter. A broken-down and vandalised fork lift truck wallowed in tall weeds like the hulk of a dead dinosaur.

The rain rattled on the roof and bounced like marbles off the hard ground. A few water-veiled yards away the rain-troubled surface of the river looked like it was boiling.

'I'm Beth,' Beth told the woman. 'And he's Hal.'

'My name's Pavane Hornby,' said the young woman.

'You're sure there isn't someone else working with you?' Beth asked, remembering the two grey figures she'd seen earlier.

'We always work alone,' Pavane said. 'Why do you ask?'

'I thought I saw two of you earlier,' Beth said. 'And Hal took a picture of *two* kookie-looking people standing down on the beach that night.'

Pavane shook her head. 'I don't know who you saw, Beth – but it wasn't me.'

'Maybe it was some other Seventh Wave

people?' Beth said. 'They looked a lot like you did in your alien mask.'

'They weren't from Seventh Wave,' Pavane said firmly.

'Well, that sure is weird,' Beth muttered.

'Excuse me, but Horace Downey just ordered a guy called Richard MacNamarra to *shoot* us!' Hal shouted above the constant noise of the rain. 'And the MacNamarra guy and another guy called Drew just went out with another load of barrels to dump them in the bay.'

'Yes, I saw them,' Pavane said. She gave the two friends a triumphant grin. 'This is all the evidence we needed!' she said. She pulled a mobile phone out of a pocket in her sweatshirt. 'I'll just call my friends and we'll have the police over here ready to arrest those two guys the moment they show up again.' As she pressed out a number, she looked at Hal and Beth. 'How did you get involved in all this?' she asked. 'Don't you know how dangerous this all is?'

Beth spluttered with speechless indignation. Of course they knew how dangerous it all was! Did Pavane think they were dumb, or what?

'It's a long story,' Hal said.

'Tell me – how come you're so strong?' Beth asked Pavane.

'I work out,' Pavane said. 'I have a black belt in *haku shim*.' She frowned and punched out the phone number again. 'Damn!' she spat.

'Problem?' Beth asked.

'The phone's dead. I don't know if it's the battery or the weather conditions, but I can't get anything out of it.' She slid the useless phone back into her pocket.

'No problem,' she said, 'we'll just have to improvise.' She looked at Hal and Beth. 'How long would it take you to get to the police?'

'If we run like crazy over the footbridge, we could be there in maybe ten minutes, I guess,' Hal said.

Pavane gnawed at her thumbnail. 'Ten minutes there,' she muttered, peering through the cascades of rain water that flooded off the sloped metal roof of their shelter. 'Maybe five minutes for the police to get their act together. Say, a quarter of an hour to get back here – they'll have to use the main road and cross the bridge up-river. That's half an hour.' She seemed to be thinking aloud. 'Will that give us enough time to have them lying in wait when the boat gets back?'

'It should be plenty of time,' Beth said. 'The boat must have been out there for an hour or more last night.'

'Yeah, but Drew was pouring the stuff out of the barrels last night,' Hal said. 'This time they're just going to dump the barrels over the side. Even if they go out beyond Cranberry Island, they could easily be back here in half an hour.'

'Then we'll just have to run *faster*,' Beth said.

'No, wait!' Pavane said. 'We need to make a contingency plan in case they get back before the police arrive. We need to set up some kind of a trap.' She looked at the two friends. 'Who's the fastest runner?'

'I am,' Hal said.

'OK, you go get the police,' Pavane said. 'Beth? Will you stay and help me?'

'Sure thing,' Beth said. 'I'll really enjoy getting my own back on that creep MacNamarra. I want to see the look on his face when he walks right into a trap!'

Pavane smiled grimly. 'I wasn't planning on us being that close,' she said. 'Not if he's armed.'

'I'll see you guys later,' Hal said. He paused for a second at the edge of the shelter, gathering his strength, then he sprinted off into the rain. Beth and Pavane watched as he jumped over obstacles in the pelting rain, mud kicking up behind him. His running figure was already becoming grey and misty as he reached the wooden footbridge and started across it.

A flash of lightning lit up the sky for a second and there was another titanic clap of thunder. Beth crammed her fingers in her ears. Pavane shouted something at her.

'What?' Beth yelled back.

Pavane yanked Beth's arms down from the sides of her head. 'I said, let's get to work.'

'Right! What's the plan?'

Pavane stared over toward the warehouse where the remaining few barrels were stored. 'Did you see any other way in or out of there?' she asked Beth. She pointed. 'Other than that door?'

'I don't think so,' Beth said. 'Nope. I'm pretty sure that was it.'

'OK,' Pavane said. 'Here's what we do. We find ourselves a big hunk of timber.'

'Right!' Beth said. 'And when they get back we whack 'em with it, right?'

'No, we don't *whack* them,' Pavane said with a small grin. 'We keep out of sight until they're both in the building. Then we use the hunk of timber to hold the door closed. And then we hope the cops arrive before they manage to break out.'

'Uh, the door opens *inwards*,' Beth pointed out. 'So how do we wedge it shut?'

'By shoving the piece of wood through the handle,' Pavane said. 'See? There's a loop. We could easily ram a chunk of board through there.' Beth peered into the rain. Pavane was right. The handle on the outside of the door was a big old loop of iron. A length of clapboard or floorboard *could* be fed through it, so long as the people doing the feeding were quick, and so long as the two men inside the warehouse didn't figure what was going on and kick their way out before the block was secure.

'OK,' Beth said, looking around the shelter. 'Let's find ourselves a piece of timber.' The back wall was made of badly-laid clapboard. Beth clambered over weed-choked pieces of machinery to take a better look.

Plenty of the boards looked about ready to fall off.

'Wait up,' Pavane said. 'Don't start hauling at stuff until I say so. I don't want this whole thing collapsing on top of us.'

'No sweat,' Beth said. 'I've got it covered.' She jumped up and caught hold of a hanging end of timber. It looked loose enough to just come away in her hands. Except that it didn't.

It bent and twisted under her weight and Beth found herself hanging unexpectedly with both feet off the ground. She swung on the board with all her weight, trying to wrench it free.

'Beth! Be careful!' Pavane yelled as the whole structure shuddered.

Suddenly it felt to Beth like the whole world had gotten up and shaken itself. She heard a cracking and a groaning noise, and there was the rush and crash of falling wood and metal as the ramshackle shelter keeled over.

Beth just had time to glance up and see a heavy sheet of roofing iron falling toward her, before something cannoned into her side and sent her sprawling out face-first in the mud.

She covered her head as she heard the fragile construction collapse completely.

She dashed the muddy water out of her eyes. The humped back of the old fork lift truck protruded through the sheets of corrugated iron and pieces of timber.

'Pavane!' she screamed, stumbling forward. A limp hand stuck out from under the debris. In saving Beth, Pavane had taken the full force of the crashing roof on her head.

15

Don't panic! This is no time to panic!

What do you mean? This is the *perfect* time to panic!

Somehow, the emergency lent Beth unexpected strength. Almost without conscious thought, she gripped the lip of the sheet of iron, and, bracing herself, she hauled upwards.

With a rush and a clang, she jerked the debris away from Pavane's still form. Beth's mother's voice sounded in her mind, leading her through the first aid procedure for unconscious accident victims.

Beth checked that Pavane was breathing. Yes! And there was no blood and no obvious external sign of injury. It just looked like the metal had struck her on the head and knocked her out.

Beth's legs gave way under her with relief and she found herself sitting in a nest of thick mud as the rain poured over her.

But she quickly recovered. She eased Pavane into the proper first aid *coma position*. She should be safe enough now, until Beth could go get help.

But that was the problem. What was Beth to do? She couldn't just run across into New Greenwich and leave Pavane like that. What if Richard MacNamarra and Drew got back and found her?

Beth only took a few seconds to make her mind up. She dragged some debris from the fallen shelter around in front of Pavane, so she couldn't be seen from the wharf. And then it was time for Beth to do the only thing she *could* do in the circumstances. She selected a length of sound timber from the wreckage, jerked it loose and dragged it through the mud over to the warehouse.

She leaned up against the side wall of the building, out of sight of the wharf. She stood the board up beside her and waited.

Every now and then, she imagined she heard the faint throb of the returning motorboat. It was on one of these occasions, as she peered around the corner of the building and strained her eyes into the running river mouth, that she spotted something that had been obvious all along.

The warehouse door was ajar. They'd forgotten

to close it again after their escape. That would be the first thing Richard MacNamarra would notice when he got back.

Beth splashed through the mud and hauled the heavy door closed. It was hard to keep a foothold in the slithery red mud and she nearly lost her footing as the door thudded shut.

Above the constant sound of the rain, Beth heard something. A low, throaty, grumbling roar. She snapped her head around and stared with rain-filled eyes down toward the ocean.

A small nub of darkness was nosing forward through the water. The boat was coming back.

Move it, Beth! she muttered to herself. But as she turned to run for cover, her foot caught on something – a chunk of rock or a piece of junk in the mud. She tumbled, full-length, into the mud, skidding along on her face.

'Urrrgh!' Her mouth was full of mud. It was in her eyes and in her ears and down inside her clothes. It was *everywhere*.

But there wasn't *time* to clean up. Coughing and spitting, Beth hauled herself to her hands and knees and scuttled around the corner of the warehouse like a bug escaping a bug-eating-bird.

She dragged herself to a sitting position against the side wall. She tried to control her breathing so that she could hear the approaching boat. Pretty soon she didn't need to hold her breath any more – the roar of the motor reached a crescendo and she heard the hollow bump of the bows against the wharf. Then she heard Richard MacNamarra's voice, although she couldn't make out what he was saying.

She created a mental picture of the two men. They climbed out of the boat. They moored it. They walked toward the warehouse door. They opened it. They went inside.

Beth snatched a look around the corner.

'Yess!' As she looked she saw the two bulky, rain-swept figures pushing the door open. She knew she only had a few seconds now before they saw that she and Hal were missing.

She jumped up and snatched at the board. It was heavy and unwieldy, and she could only stagger along with it balanced precariously in her arms.

The forward end of the board jammed itself against the ground and when she yanked back to get it loose she nearly fell over again as her feet skidded under her.

This was turning into a total nightmare. And

things didn't improve when she realized she'd have to drop the board in order to pull the door closed. And then she'd have to hold the door closed against the two men while she tried to insert the board through the handle-loop.

Yeah, and like they'll be standing there twiddling their thumbs while I'm doing all this!

She came to the door just as one of the heavily-suited men lumbered out. She was too late. They'd seen that the captives had escaped.

She caught a glimpse of Drew's face through the visor. And then some kind of protective instinct took over. Almost without being aware of what she was doing, Beth swung the heavy board straight at Drew's midriff.

Whack!

The impact of the board sent Drew staggering backwards. He cannoned into Richard MacNamarra and the two of them went crashing to the ground inside the warehouse like a pair of tenpins.

If not for the cumbersome protective suits, the two men would probably have been back on their feet and all over Beth before she could have moved. But as it was, they struggled on the ground like a couple of upended beetles.

With a shout of triumph, Beth dropped the board and wrenched the door closed. A second later, she had the board in her arms again and was trying to shove the wavering end through the handle. It was like trying to thread a needle with your eyes closed and with boxing gloves on! The board just wouldn't behave itself. It was just too heavy for Beth to control.

Then the worst happened. She heard the thump of someone grabbing the handle on the inside, and the door began to move inwards.

The door was a fraction open when Beth finally managed to get the end of the board through the iron loop. She charged sideways, sliding the board along the door and across the warehouse wall.

The door thwacked closed.

Beth lost her footing again and splattered into the mud. But she'd done it! The warehouse door was well and truly blocked off.

While she was still scraping mud out of her eyes, Beth heard the splash-sploosh of running feet. For a moment she thought the two men had found a second way out and were coming to get her. But then she saw police uniforms.

'In there!' she hollered, waving her arms. 'They're in there!'

She was plucked up out of the mud and set on wobbly legs.

'OK,' a reassuring voice said. 'Good girl! We'll handle this from here on in.'

Someone else took hold of her by the shoulders and she was led around to the side of the warehouse.

She scooped more mud off her face. In a gap between two sheds she could see the revolving blue light of a police car. Another police officer ran past her, his gun in his hand.

Hal came running up to her.

'Are you OK?' he gasped. 'Where's Pavane?'

'Over here!' Beth yelled. She led Officer Perch over to where the young woman lay.

'What happened to her?' Hal asked as Officer Perch knelt at Pavane's side. Right on cue, Pavane groaned and moved. She was coming round.

Beth shot Hal a glance. 'She had an accident,' she said. 'I'll explain later.'

There were shouts from behind them and the two friends looked around to see Richard MacNamarra and Drew Bacchus, shed of their protective suits, being marched at gunpoint to the waiting police car.

Pavane got to her feet. She seemed woozy but not too badly hurt considering she'd had a shed fall on her.

Beth and Hal looked at each other and smiled.

'You sure are muddy,' Hal said.

Beth grinned a bright grin through a mask of mud. 'And you sure are wet,' she said.

There were plenty of people gathered around the Hunters' living room fire a few nights later. Beth and her mom were there. So was Beth's gran and nearly all the Moon family – minus only Don Moon, who was still on location, and Joe, who was doing something with his motorbike, as ever.

They also had a guest of honour. Pavane Hornby had come to visit, and to listen as Beth stood with her back to the first real log fire of the fall and read out the report in The Clarion.

'"If not for the intelligence and quick thinking of Hal Moon and his friend Beth Hunter, the two men would in all likelihood have gotten clean away and there would have been no substantive proof that Webcore had been involved in the clandestine disposal of untreated toxic chemical waste."'

'Substantive proof?' Beth's gran muttered. 'Clandestine disposal? I wish they'd make an effort to be understood. A person could choke to death on some of those words.'

'It just means that Beth and Hal helped uncover

161

the biggest scandal to hit this area for a very long time,' Beth's mom said proudly. 'Apparently the FBI had been suspicious about Webcore for some time. They were told there was something criminal going on there by the environmental group that Pavane belongs to.'

'That's right,' Pavane added, 'but there wasn't enough evidence to prove what they were up to, and the FBI couldn't afford to upset a big-shot like Horace Downey unless they could make charges stick.'

'It's a real shame that Downey had the chance to go into hiding before he was caught,' Hal said.

The full report of the incident had revealed that Mr Downey's mansion had been deserted when the FBI agents had broken in. The wicked old man hadn't been seen since.

'That's right,' Pavane said. 'MacNamarra and Bacchus were just following his orders. The old guy is probably in South America by now!'

'Yeah, but if not for your people in Seventh Wave,' Hal pointed out, 'Webcore might not have been stopped at all! So it's not like you failed or anything.'

Pavane nodded. 'That's right. At least Webcore has been stopped.' She smiled grimly. 'I guess that means we can get to work on the *next* problem.'

'I just wish that horrible old man hadn't taken our pictures,' Beth said. 'That was the only proof we had that there might be real *aliens* out there!'

'Beth!' her mom said warningly. 'There weren't any *aliens*, OK?'

'We saw *something*,' Hal said quietly. '*Two* somethings.'

'Maybe,' Mrs Hunter said, 'but it wasn't little men from another planet! I don't want to hear any more of this nonsense from either of you! Aliens! Good grief!'

'I guess I'd better be making tracks,' Pavane said.

'You don't have to go right this minute, surely?' Beth said. 'You've got time for some food before you go, huh? I've been baking all afternoon.' She got up and headed for the kitchen. 'Everyone's to have a slice!' she called.

Two minutes later she came back in bearing a laden tray.

'It's a secret recipe,' she said as she set the tray down on the coffee table. 'Only two people in the entire world know how to bake it: my gran and I.'

It was on a big dish. It was brown and goey and lumpy and sticky. It was Beth's first ever attempt at Ugly Cake.

Everyone agreed that it was the most delicious Ugly Cake they'd ever eaten. Even gran said she couldn't have done it any better.

Beth sat on the floor in front of the fire and licked the thick chocolate sauce off her lips. 'You know,' she said thoughtfully, 'there are only two things that bother me about this whole business.'

'Really, Beth?' Mrs Moon asked as she spooned more chocolate goo into baby Ben's thoroughly chocolatey mouth. 'What are they?'

Beth held a finger up. 'First, I think the newspaper should have put *Beth Hunter and Hal Moon* instead of *Hal Moon and Beth Hunter*, and second, I wish Pavane had been a real alien!' She grinned. 'Then everything would have been just *perfect*!'

Later that night, Beth was lying in bed reading Hal's *Darkwood Incident* book, when there was a soft tap on her door.

'Come in,' she called. Her gran slid into the room and sat on the edge of Beth's bed.

'I just came to say goodnight,' Gran said.

Beth smiled fondly at her. 'Did I do good with the Ugly Cake?' she asked.

Gran touched her fingertips to her pursed lips

and made a kissing sound. 'You made it perfect, Beth. Now I know the ancient recipe is in good hands.'

'I thought Mom said you made the recipe up yourself,' Beth said with a smile. 'So how come it's *ancient* all of a sudden?'

Gran proudly patted her chest. 'Because I'm ancient,' she said with a laugh. Her face became serious and she leaned toward Beth. 'There's something else I want to tell you.' She glanced at the door as if she expected to see Mrs Hunter's ear come straining around the narrow gap. 'Remember that talk we had the other day about seeing people from outer space?'

'Uh-huh,' Beth breathed.

'When I was a girl,' Gran said, 'not much older than you are now, I was walking in the forest over near Darkwood one Sunday afternoon when something happened that I've not mentioned to anyone for years.' She patted Beth's knee through the bed covers. 'Everyone said I was crazy, anyway,' she said. 'So I stopped talking about it. I've never mentioned it to your mother, either.' Gran shook her head. 'Karen would never have believed me. She's too narrow-minded. Always has been. Not like you and I, Beth.'

'What wouldn't Mom have believed you about?'

Beth breathed in an ecstacy of suspense. 'What happened?'

'I saw a little person from another planet,' Gran whispered. 'Everyone said I had hair on my teeth, you know? But I guess you're maybe the one person in the world who'll believe me. It was a little fellow, no bigger than I was at the time, and he had huge black eyes and little spindly arms and legs. And . . .'

'Mom?' Mrs Hunter's face appeared around Beth's bedroom door. 'I thought I heard voices.' She looked from Beth to Gran. 'So? What's going on in here, huh?' She grinned. 'It looks like a conspiracy to me.'

Gran smiled. She leaned forward and kissed Beth on the forehead.

'I was just telling our little heroine goodnight, that's all,' she said. 'Goodnight and sleep tight.' She stood up. 'And now I'm about ready to hit the hay.'

'Gran?' Beth called. 'Can we talk some more about . . . uh . . . that *thing* we were talking about?'

Gran smiled as she joined Beth's mom at the door. 'Sure we can,' she said. 'We can have plenty of talks. Goodnight, sweetheart.'

'Goodnight, Beth,' Mrs Hunter said. 'Don't be

too long before you turn the light out, OK? You need your sleep after all that excitement.'

Beth nodded.

Sleep? Like, a person was expected to *sleep* after what Beth had just been told? As she lay there in her warm bed, listening to the faint swish of the ocean on the sand and the murmur of the wind through the leaves of the New England fall, it was all too easy for her to imagine silver machines hidden in the woods and slim, pale figures sliding silently through the trees. And one day, Beth was absolutely determined, *one day* she was going to *see* an alien just like her gran had done all those years ago.

And she wouldn't stop looking until she *did* see one! And that was a promise!

THE WEIRD EYES FILE
A Hunter & Moon Mystery

Allan Frewin Jones

Meet next door neighbours, Beth Hunter and Hal Moon. Beth's imagination's always getting her into trouble and Hal's practical jokes always backfire . . . but when mystery stares them in the face, Hunter & Moon are on the case!

Beth disturbs a burglar outside her room. What was he after? She's got nothing of value. There's no sign of a break-in and nothing's been taken. The police don't believe her – was her imagination playing tricks? Only one *weird* pair of eyes saw what *really* happened . . .

Another Hodder Children's book

THE SKULL STONE FILE
A Hunter & Moon Mystery

Allan Frewin Jones

Meet next door neighbours, Beth Hunter and Hal Moon. Beth's imagination's always getting her into trouble and Hal's practical jokes always backfire . . . but when mystery stares them in the face, Hunter & Moon are on the case!

Beth's taken an instant dislike to a skull carving Hal's bought locally – she's got a thing about skulls – so it's banished outside. But overnight the skull stone explodes – cracking open to reveal a cryptic message.

A message that leads them through the snow-capped forests, across ancient Indian burial grounds – and into a whole lot of trouble . . .

THE SECRET ROOM SLEEPOVER

Sharon Siamon

Are you sitting comfortably . . . ? Jo has a very strange story to tell. Will it scare easy-going Alex? Louise is terrified of ghosts, but loves a sleepover. And Charlie loves junk food — a sleepover is the perfect excuse! Safely settled in the cosy cellar of Jo's old house, the sleepover gang snuggle down to listen . . .

Once a richly furnished bedroom, now all was dust and decay. Diana glimpsed a wavering shape in the mirror behind her, reaching. A chill terror swept through her. Who did the room belong to? Why must it not be disturbed? And what will happen to Diana now?

ORDER FORM

HUNTER AND MOON MYSTERIES
Allan Frewin Jones

0 340 67818 6	THE WEIRD EYES FILE	£3.50	❏
0 340 67819 4	THE ALIEN FIRE FILE	£3.50	❏
0 340 67820 8	THE SKULL STONE FILE	£3.50	❏

THE SLEEPOVER SERIES
Sharon Siamon

0 340 67276 5	THE SECRET ROOM SLEEPOVER	£3.50	❏
0 340 67277 3	THE SNOWED-IN SLEEPOVER	£3.50	❏

All Hodder Children's books are available at your local bookshop or newsagent, or can be ordered direct from the publisher. Just tick the titles you want and fill in the form below. Prices and availability subject to change without notice.

Hodder Children's Books, Cash Sales Department, Bookpoint, 39 Milton Park, Abingdon, OXON, OX14 4TD, UK. If you have a credit card you may order by telephone – (01235) 831700.

Please enclose a cheque or postal order made payable to Bookpoint Ltd to the value of the cover price and allow the following for postage and packing:
UK & BFPO – £1.00 for the first book, 50p for the second book, and 30p for each additional book ordered up to a maximum charge of £3.00.
OVERSEAS & EIRE – £2.00 for the first book, £1.00 for the second book, and 50p for each additional book.

Name...

Address...

....

....

If you would prefer to pay by credit card, please complete:
Please debit my Visa/Access/Diner's Card/American Express (delete as applicable) card no:

Signature...

Expiry Date...